"With chilling specificity, Arnoldi describes every chiseled, hypodermic-penetrated inch of Aurora's abused, pumped-up body and the monstrous metamorphosis she ultimately suffers, one that pushes the boundaries of health, gender, humanness, and sanity. Arnoldi's searing tale, a true binge read, boldly dramatizes the consequences of narcissism and misplaced ambition."

—*Booklist*

"Arnoldi shows herself to be an impeccable, and sometimes lyrical, authority on the world she describes, providing litanies of the obsessions that gym rats develop—the work regimens, the growth drugs, the nauseating side effects—all juxtaposed with fastidious descriptions of Charles's sexual performances, where thrusts are counted like weightlifters' reps."

—*Kirkus Reviews*

"*Chemical Pink* relentlessly fuses (and confuses) attitude about food, body, gender, sexuality, family, celebrity, and ambition until everything from a plate of steak to another human being becomes an object of consumption."

—*Paper* magazine

"It is difficult these days to shock and beguile with a kind of aggressive innocence, but Miss Arnoldi has in this book. It is disturbingly funny and utterly unflinching."

—Susanna Moore, author of *In the Cut*

"Darkly hilarious."

—*Talk* magazine

CHEMICAL Pink

KATIE ARNOLDI

A Tom Doherty Associates Book

New York

CHEMICAL PINK

Copyright © 2001 by Katie Arnoldi

This book is printed on acid-free paper.

A Forge Book
Published by Tom Doherty Associates, LLC
175 Fifth Avenue
New York, NY 10010

www.tor.com

Forge® is a registered trademark of Tom Doherty Associates, LLC.

Library of Congress Cataloging-in-Publication Data

Arnoldi, Katie.
    Chemical pink / Katie Arnoldi.
        p. cm.
    "A Tom Doherty Associates book."
    ISBN 0-312-87450-2 (hc)
    ISBN 0-312-87891-5 (pbk)
        1. Women bodybuilders—Fiction. 2. Eccentrics and eccentricities—
Fiction. 3. Man-woman relationships—Fiction. 4. Control (Psychology)—
Fiction. 5. Body image—Fiction. 6. California—Fiction. I. Title.

PS3551.R555 C47 2001
813'.6—dc21   00-049023

First Hardcover Edition: March 2001
First Trade Paperback Edition: April 2002

Printed in the United States of America

0 9 8 7 6 5 4 3 2 1

I dedicate this book to love of my life,
Chuck Arnoldi and to
Jamie Thompson Stern, a true friend.

ACKNOWLEDGMENTS

The following people helped make this book happen and I'd like to thank them from the bottom of my heart:

Rob Roberge, a great teacher and friend, without whom this book would never have been written. Celia Piazza read my pages every day, encouraged me and was always honest. John Burnham, one of my dearest friends and greatest supporter, helped me every step of the way. Charles Glass, the best training partner in the world, shared his incredible wealth of knowledge and inspired me to write this book. Phillip Goglia added invaluable technical advice, humor and showed great patience in meeting with me week after week. I must thank my amazing friends, Billy Al Bengston, Jay Chiat, Nadia Ghaleb, Berta and Frank Gehry, Buck Henry, Miriam Kazdim, Fiona Lewis, Art Linson, Arne List, Rick Valente, and Edwina Von Gal who gave me confidence, encouragement and a lot of help. Special thanks to Matt Bialer who believed in this book early on and made it happen. Natalia Aponte is my wonderful editor who made my dream come true. Thanks to Joni Evans, my extraordinary agent, for her enthusiastic support.

And finally I must thank my incredible family. Without you, nothing would get done.

CHEMICAL Pink

ONE

Remembering May

It had given Charles great satisfaction to rip out the green Italian marble tub, the gold fixtures, the pale green porcelain toilet and matching bidet and to install angled mirrors, harsh overhead lighting and a six-foot-square posing platform in the center of the room. He'd turned his mother's sanctuary into a shrine for bodybuilding and had a custom-built cabinet installed to store May's drugs. There was a small refrigerator for the growth hormone and a daybed where they could relax together.

Charles flipped on the light. The room and all the mirrors were clean. Mrs. Johns kept things up even though Charles rarely came here now. He opened the glass-faced cabinet. Neatly stacked and in alphabetical order were all of May's old drugs. Aldactone, Anadrol, Anavar, Clembuteral, Cytomel, Deca-Durabolin, Halotestin, Humilane R and Humilane N, Lasix, Nolvadex, Parabolan, Primabolan Acetate, Primabolan Depot, Testosterone Propionate, Winstrol. Some had expired, but Charles couldn't bring himself to throw them away. Here too, he kept the various depilatory creams, the loofahs he used to scrub away her abundant body hair, the burlap washcloth he used on her face, the antibiotic creams for the boils on her back and inner thighs and the multiple types of synthetic thyroid that they used at the end to undo or erase the sad results of their poly-pharmaceutical adventure.

May had been a star. She was beautiful and fresh and huge. The judges loved her; she'd been on every magazine cover. If they had just stopped she would be a champion today. No one could have touched May.

When her voice got hoarse and then finally dropped, neither had been surprised. All the pros had deep voices and Charles thought it sexy. At night he would have May read to him from his financial reports, his head resting comfortably in her lap. Eyes closed, he would envision her success.

Her skin thickened and became coarse; the pores opened and became visible. Charles spent a lot of money on exotic creams in an attempt to bring back some of the softness. May was a good sport, noting how well her new skin held a tan. Neither of them considered slowing down or turning back.

Charles brought in the experts when the clitorihypertrophy set in. May was troubled by her growing clitoris, so worried that Charles wouldn't find her attractive. The doctors confirmed that the virilizing side effects of anabolic/androgenic steroids were irreversible. Charles found himself even more fascinated by May. Her hard, budding little penis compelled him. As it grew so too did his devotion, and May admitted to heightened arousal.

May was winning every contest. She had offers to guest-pose all over the world. She was in constant demand for photo shoots and was given a question-and-answer column, which Charles ghostwrote, in *Flex Magazine*. She grew bigger, harder and better.

For many months her hirsutism was manageable. A light blond down grew on her back and shoulders. Charles remembered climbing into the tub with May, three or four fresh disposable razors on hand. He'd gently soap her back and shoulders, then delicately scrape the foam and hair away. Her body was slick and after the bath he would rub her with oil and marvel at the sheen of her skin. But the hair got thicker and the follicles would become infected from ingrown hairs, erupting into enormous boils. They switched to depilatory creams that Charles applied and then loofahed off, leaving the skin very clean. They found a mild depilatory for May's face.

May was famous. It was critical that she stay in shape year-round, to keep her body fat below nine percent even off-season. She relied on Cytomel to keep her metabolism fast, to keep her lean, and diuretics to prevent water retention. It worked for almost two years and then it didn't work at all. Nothing Charles tried could stimulate May's natural thyroid. Her metabolism shut down and she blew up like a walrus. He watched helplessly as she grew enormously fat, her beard thick, her features coarse. He assured her that it didn't matter; he loved her. It didn't matter if she never competed again. He meant it. But May couldn't stand herself and she couldn't stand Charles' attention. She refused to see him and then she moved back home to Florida. Charles still sent generous monthly checks with his letters. May cashed the checks but never replied.

Charles

Liz Movino had a glorious physique with giant shoulders, a freakishly small waist and a full round gluteal area that kept Charles awake at night.

It was 9:30 in the morning. Liz usually arrived at 10:00 and Charles needed to be at the front desk when she came in. He had decided that she was the one. His next project. Very promising.

Charles dressed in his black nylon sweat suit, sat on his elephant foot stool in his closet and put on his white canvas tennis shoes and new white socks. He went into the bathroom, removed his thick tortoiseshell glasses and washed his pale, freckled face vigorously with oatmeal soap and hot water. He dried himself, put his glasses back on and rinsed his mouth with old-fashioned Listerine. His thinning hair was cut very close to his head and needed no attention. He smeared Chapstick over his thin brown lips and rushed out to the car. It was 9:35.

Charles delighted in the freshness of the sunny morning. He shuddered in excitement as he pulled out of the driveway. Today would be a new beginning, the start of a glorious relationship.

May had been the first. Beautiful May, strong and blond and

very loving. May had needed little instruction. She understood him. She had been so grateful when he got her the apartment and gave her the allowance. She was able to stop wrestling and concentrate on bodybuilding. May, in her marvelous capes and her brilliant costumes. No one had ever made Charles feel like that. So strong, powerful. He loved May, and after she was gone he felt very sad. He missed her still.

Charles pulled into the lot and saw that he was too late; Liz's beat-up gold VW Rabbit was already there. He'd just have to walk up and introduce himself. "Hello, I'm Charles Worthington," he'd say. It wouldn't matter that people would stare at him, that strangers would know his business; he could ignore them. He would ask Liz to meet with him to discuss her career and certainly she would say yes. He could offer to meet with her in the parking lot if he sensed she was uncomfortable, otherwise he'd invite her back to the house for lunch. They would dine in the garden. Charles would flatter and impress her with his historic knowledge of bodybuilding. He would serve her lovely steamed chicken and vegetables. She would like him even before he mentioned money or offered the agreement. She would love him. Yes, they would have lunch and who knows? Liz was the one.

Charles locked his car and rushed into the gym. Inside there was a vast sea of machines and it took him a moment to get his bearings. He spotted Liz over in the corner by the calf machines. She wore her pink short shorts with the matching low-back G-string leotard. You could see the gluteal muscles separate and move when she walked, and if you were close enough, you could see striations within those muscles. Her massive legs were tanned that deep unnatural brown that the girls all liked. They exploded out of her shorts, tapered down to lovely little knees and then swelled again into sharply defined calves. Her back and arms were a living map of muscle. She looked beautiful in pink.

Charles walked past her, his hands buried deep in his pockets, bony shoulders hunched forward. Liz was looking down, so he kept going and climbed the stairs to the loft with stationary bikes. He got on a bike and started to pedal, not bothering to turn the thing on. Liz was talking to Louise Schultz. They had their heads close, whispering. Charles didn't like it. Louise was a freak. Her abdomen was a giant barrel etched with muscle, always bloated no matter how hard she dieted because all the growth hormone she'd taken over the years had enlarged her organs. Louise was reckless. He knew that she had to put a plastic panty shield in her posing suit so that her grotesquely exaggerated clitoris didn't show. The judges don't like to see mutant penises on women. She was short, 5'2", had a deep man's voice and terrible acne on her back. Off-season, Louise weighed in at over two hundred pounds. Liz didn't need that kind of influence. She mustn't socialize at the gym.

Liz walked over to the squat rack, loaded up a bar with forty-five-pound plates, then sat down on the bench to wrap her knees. Charles jumped off the bike and hurried down the stairs to the leg extension machine next to the squat rack. He slid into the machine, adjusted the weight stack to twenty pounds, and waited for her to look up.

"You ready, baby?" Rico said as he walked up behind Liz and rubbed her shoulders. "How you feeling?"

Rico was tall with shiny black skin, a wide back and long dreadlocks pulled back with a piece of rope. He wore a silver ring in the center of his nose, like a bull's, and had brilliant white teeth. He'd won every contest he'd entered during the last year, worked constantly as a model, and stayed lean on and off season.

They aren't together? Charles felt panicky.

"I feel good," Liz said.

"I'm gonna bust you wide open." Rico bit her lightly on her neck. "You know I am."

Liz and Rico walked over to the squat rack. Charles started doing repetitions on his machine, gripping the seat with both hands, and watching them. Liz put on her black leather weight belt with an inlay of pink snakeskin glued to the back. Did she think the belt was classy? Some sort of fashion statement? She cinched the belt tightly then took the bar off the rack, focused on her reflection in the mirror, and did her first squat. Liz barely went halfway down and Rico was there standing behind her with his large hands on her waist, helping her up.

"Nice one, baby," Rico said. "Again."

It wasn't a nice one at all. It was a partial rep. She had cheated. Charles was not impressed, plus he noticed that there was a thin layer of fat on the backs of her thighs just below the bottom of her shorts. He watched and did his own repetitions. His thin quadriceps were beginning to burn. Liz dropped into her second squat, this time deeper, and got stuck at the bottom.

"Stand up, goddamn it," yelled Rico. "Quitter? Get up, bitch."

Liz stood up and immediately went into another squat, this time deep and perfect. She did four more and then racked the bar.

"We're building the world's best damn ass," Rico said.

Liz smiled, wiped her nose on the back of her hand, and hugged Rico, forcing her pelvis into his bulging crotch. Rico grabbed a handful of her hair and yanked her head to his, kissing her on the mouth, his other hand exploring the sweat-damp area between her legs. Charles climbed off his machine and walked quickly past the couple, toward the exit.

Outside there were filthy newspapers and old food containers, rotting fruit and dog shit on the sidewalk and in the gutter. Venice was a hellhole. Charles crossed the street and walked two blocks to the ocean, bought a cold bottle of water at the liquor store, and sat on the concrete bench facing the beach. It was a hot day but Charles didn't consider taking off his black nylon sweatshirt. He sipped the water and gazed out at the sand and the bodies baking in the sun. This was a wide beach, the ocean so far from him that he couldn't hear the small waves breaking on the shore. It was quiet here. This was the place the bodybuilders came to. They didn't read at this beach; they tanned, applied lotion and listened to music. They didn't swim. He'd never seen a bodybuilder actually go into the water. Here men and women wore G-strings displaying their giant brown buttocks. During the winter when the beach was more deserted Charles had seen a couple of the women go topless. Now that summer was coming, all the girls had their nipples covered by tiny triangles of fabric.

May had loved it here. Charles used to come and sit on the bench, sometimes with an umbrella if it was very hot, and May would spread her towel in front of him. He would watch her while she tanned.

Today there were some new people at the beach. Charles didn't recognize several of the girls and a couple of them were quite nice. As he sat and watched them bake, he felt better. He would find out the name of the blond in the red suit and also that dark-haired girl with the big deltoids. He finished his water and walked back to the gym.

Joey, the gym manager, said the blond was Aurora Jeanine Johnson. She'd added the Aurora when she won the Southern States Bodybuilding Championship. She was twenty-nine, had a twelve-year-old daughter back home in Savannah, and was here alone on vacation for two weeks, training at Gold's Gym. She stayed at the Marina Pacific Hotel and usually worked out around eight o'clock in the morning and then again at four. The dark-haired girl was named Betty. She was a lesbian, and her girlfriend was a lawyer named Joan. That was all the information Joey had. Charles thanked him, handed him the usual tightly folded twenty-dollar bill and rushed back out to his car.

Ready

Charles' house was on a hill, set in a grove of tall old lemon eucalyptus trees. The trunks of the trees were very white and smooth, and where the branches curved the bark bunched and wrinkled like skin. Some of the trees split into two thick limbs that resembled legs. Charles liked to sit outside in his garden and admire his trees. He liked to press his cheeks and hands to the trunks and feel their coolness. He liked to scrape the white bark with a knife just to see the green raw flesh underneath. When he cut the tree like that it left a permanent scar and he didn't do it often, although each tree bore his mark.

The massive wooden house was stained a rich deep brown. It had a dark shingled roof, large beams and heavy wooden doors. The upstairs bedrooms all had wrought iron balconies and from most rooms you could see the ocean. Charles had lived here all his life. When his mother died five years before, he threw away all the family photos and had Mrs. Johns, the housekeeper, take most of his mother's clothes. He gave away her bed and the furniture in her room and turned her bedroom into a storage area. He sold her jewelry, even the family pieces. He had all the furniture cleaned and the pillows sprayed with a deodorizer to rid the house of her smell. He took his mother's paintings and donated them to the museum. Paintings of insipid-looking English women, with weak delicate hands laid on their breast, looking off into space or English valleys with streams and trees and flowers, large sailing ships with the captain at the helm. The Elizabethan dining room chairs were sold back to the antiques dealer; her books were donated to the library that bore her name. He threw out all the chutney and biscuits and fruit preserves in the pantry, all the food in the freezer.

"Shall I serve your lunch in the garden today?" asked the ancient Mrs. Johns when Charles came in.

"That would be fine, thank you." Charles rushed past her and up the back stairway.

The bookshelves in Charles' room went from floor to ceiling and covered the east wall. Here he kept his collection of body-building magazines—every issue of every magazine for the last five years, American, European and Japanese. The earlier copies he stored in his mother's old bedroom. Charles pulled the 1995 October and November issues of *Women's Physique World* and *Muscle Mag* and quickly found the articles on the Southern States Contest. There she was, Jeannie Johnson, heavyweight and over-all winner, in her bright yellow posing suit. Jeannie, now Aurora, in a front double bicep with her right leg extended to the side and her fabulous quadriceps alive and rippling. A side chest pose before she got her breast implants. The implants aided her symmetry. Charles was surprised he hadn't noticed her before. She was splendid. He spent another hour going through the magazines looking for more information on Aurora but there were very few articles. He found a couple of profiles that talked about her training techniques and an interview, in which she did not mention her daughter. Apparently she hadn't competed since

1995. Probably she'd been working at putting on size and from what he'd seen on the beach she was quite thick. He stacked the magazines neatly on his bedside table, then showered and changed for lunch.

Charles had always been frail, with a delicate stomach. As a child he'd been allergic to dairy, nuts, shellfish and wheat. He could tolerate wheat and dairy now but nuts and shellfish gave him hives. He was frequently constipated and even mildly spicy food gave him heartburn. He needed to be careful with his foods.

Today for lunch Mrs. Johns had prepared cream of carrot soup with toast points, chicken salad nestled in butter lettuce, and for dessert sliced banana mixed with her freshly stewed prunes. Charles tucked his napkin into his shirt collar, as was his habit when he ate alone. Vouvou, his wheezing English bulldog, joined him in the garden and sat next to his chair drooling and begging. Charles rang the silver bell that sat next to his water glass and summoned Mrs. Johns.

"Please bring Vouvou a little bowl of chicken. She's very hungry," Charles said.

An auburn net held Mrs. Johns' brittle gray hair firmly in place. She'd been with Charles' family all his life; first as a nanny, then as a housekeeper. She came three times a week to clean house. Mrs. Johns put her spotted, twisted hands on her bony hips, shook her head. "That dog is very fat."

"Just a small bowl." Charles took a sip of water and patted Vouvou on the head.

Mrs. Johns sighed, lurched inside in her slow skeletal gait, and brought Vouvou a chicken breast cut into small pieces. Charles set the dog's food down next to his chair and ate all of his lunch.

Go

It was 4:30 and Aurora still had not arrived at the gym. Charles was getting tired of pedaling the stationary bike. Even with the power turned off he was perspiring. Sitting next to him, dripping sweat all over the floor, was Baron Hacker, "The Bat." He had all his publicity photographs taken in a Batman mask and cape; had the Batman logo painted on his weight belt, gym bag and car; and was frequently seen wearing a black cape. Baron had his headphones on and was singing loudly, off key. Every now and then he waved his arms to the rhythm of the song or else played an elaborate set of invisible drums, showering Charles and the area around him with his wetness.

Down on the floor the after-work crowd was beginning to assemble. Skinny secretaries with highlighted hair wearing striped bell-bottomed tights and high-heeled tennis shoes and matching bra-tops, their makeup thick with darkly painted lips, mingled with young executives with thinning hair who walked around with their bike shorts underneath their basketball shorts and their baseball caps and the fancy shoes. These young professionals shouted and hugged and slapped each other's backs. White guys who called each other "Brother" or "G." These were

average people with the distorted attitudes of world-class athletes. Charles found them utterly uninteresting and was about to
leave when he saw Aurora walk in, dressed all in white. She was
a vision. Charles got off the bike and went down onto the gym
floor to get a better look. She stood by the pull-down machine
putting on her gloves when he walked up.

"Aurora Johnson?"

"Yes," she said and smiled. Charles was delighted to see that
she was even prettier in person. She had lovely full lips, a delicate—almost aristocratic—nose and nice, straight, white teeth.
Healthy gums.

"Charles Worthington." He extended his hand. "I've been
following your career for some time now."

"Thank you." She grasped his hand and squeezed hard, hurt-
ing him a little.

"You looked sensational at the Southern States." He gently
withdrew his hand.

"I was lucky." She looked down, shyly, and adjusted the wrist
strap on her glove. "The competition's a lot tougher out here."

"You'd stand out anywhere," Charles said, touching her
cleanly shaved forearm. "Trust me."

"Thank you, Charles." Aurora smiled and her face lit up.
Her skin was clear, not a trace of acne. "It's very nice to meet
you."

"I'll let you train. Have a great workout." Charles walked
out to his car smiling.

That night he dreamed of dressing his penis in a kimono and
a matching bonnet with a lovely geisha girl's face drawn on the
head. His penis sang to him and brought him great joy. In the
morning Charles awoke refreshed, happy and well rested. He
dressed quickly and left the house before Mrs. Johns arrived.

The coffee shop at the Marina Pacific Hotel opened off the
lobby. Charles got a table with a good view of the elevator and

ordered coffee. At 7:45 the elevator door opened and Aurora stepped out. Charles put the money for his coffee on the table and strolled into the lobby.

"Aurora," he said in his surprised tone. "Hello."

Her face opened into a wide smile. "Charles. You staying here too?"

"No. I just had breakfast. Food's good. On my way to the gym. Give you a ride somewhere?"

"That'd be great. I'm going to the gym too."

Charles and Aurora walked out and climbed into his big white Mercedes.

First Date

Charles wore his black wool crepe suit with black crocodile loafers and cashmere socks. He'd filed and buffed his nails, had given his ears an extra-good cleaning, and felt ready for anything. He held the door open for Aurora and watched as she teetered past him in her cheap, red, clunky high heels. He had an urge to grab her fine round ass, run his thumbs down the crack between her cheeks and yank the flimsy spandex dress over her head. He wanted to have a look. Instead he smiled and took Aurora's arm, steadying her, and guided her into the restaurant.

"This place is beautiful," Aurora said a little too loudly. She stood there in the entry, looking around, her hands clutching her cheap silver rhinestone evening purse. Charles noticed the large party at the first table look up and stare at Aurora. They whispered amongst themselves.

"Good evening, Mr. Worthington," said the maître d'. "Nice to see you."

"Hello, Stuart."

"This way, please."

Charles took Aurora's elbow and guided her through the maze of tables. He was delighted to see that every person they passed looked up and was struck by Aurora, often nudging or kicking their dinner partners. The maître d' pulled out the chair and Charles helped her settle in, reluctantly releasing her elbow and taking his seat.

"God, this is nice." Aurora picked up her menu, and Charles saw that one of her long red nails was slightly chipped. It fasci nated him that so many of these competitive bodybuilders, who lifted so much weight, whose hands were so rough and calloused, managed to maintain extraordinarily long nails and keep them neatly painted. A lovely feminine touch.

"It's the only restaurant I patronize," Charles said. "Food's outstanding. You'll be able to eat here."

"Great," she said. "I'm going off the diet tonight."

"You can eat perfectly clean."

"But I don't want to."

Charles reached across the table and touched her arm. "I'm glad we met." He traced the veins in her forearm with his fingers.

Aurora nodded. "That was lucky, seeing you at the hotel." She watched Charles touch her. "Didn't think I'd meet anybody. They're not real friendly out here."

"Some of the girls are pretty disagreeable," Charles said.

"Guys are worse. Grabbing and joking. That Rico, second day I was here, walks up and tells me he would consider 'doing me.' "

"I'm sorry." Charles squeezed her hand. "A lot of undesira- bles in that gym. You have to ignore those types and focus on what you're doing."

"I guess." She removed her hand from Charles' and raked it through her fiercely teased and frosted blond hair. Charles mar- veled at the separation of the tricep and bicep muscles, the full- ness of her front and side delts, and at how well she'd achieved an even tan on her arms and armpits.

"At home I'm a big deal," she said. "There's no one in Georgia. But I can't stand next to these girls."

"Good evening, Mr. Worthington," Allen interrupted as he walked up to the table. "Would you like to hear our specials?"

"No thank you, Allen," Charles said. "The ahi and steamed spinach. Four or six ounces, Aurora?"

"Six would be great," she said, and smiled at the waiter.

"You have the genetics." Charles pulled the car away from the restaurant out into traffic. "That's the main thing. The rest can be achieved."

"I don't know." Aurora turned in her seat to face him, one knee bent and on the seat, the other straight, forcing the dress up toward her hips, nearly revealing her panties. "I've never been as hard as, say, Lenore Gibbs. No matter what I do. I stand next to her and I look tiny, flat and soft."

"Lenore has access to a wide array of pharmaceuticals."

"Yeah."

"Lenore also has a contract with Weider," Charles said, stopping the car at the light and turning to Aurora, forcing himself to look in her eyes and not at her crotch. "She's free to focus completely on her training."

"That must be nice," she said. "Instead of bills and school lunches."

Charles pulled into the small driveway of the Marina Pacific Hotel. He put the car in Park, leaving the engine on. "I've enjoyed our time."

They both sat still for a moment.

Aurora turned to face him. "Would you like to come up? My room's not much, but we could talk more."

He turned off the ignition. "I'd like that."

*   *   *

Aurora opened the door and flipped on the light. Charles followed, watching her calves clench and separate with each step.

"I wish I had more to offer you." She pulled the one chair out from the desk and faced it toward the queen bed. The seat matched the beige-and-pink seashell pattern of the bedspread. She put her purse on the table then moved it to the empty luggage rack. "All I've got is water and canned tuna."

"Water's fine."

Aurora took the two glasses on the TV and pulled off the protective plastic wrap. She filled each glass from her half-empty gallon container of distilled water and handed one to Charles, spilling a little on his hand.

"You take the chair." She tugged down her dress then sat on the bed. "Actually, I'm gonna, real quick, change." She yanked open the top drawer of the bureau and the whole thing came out, almost spilling the jumbled mess of clothes on the floor. She forced it back in and grabbed something orange.

Charles sat when Aurora closed the bathroom door. He raised his arm and sniffed at his armpit. He checked his nails, then scraped his teeth at the gum line and checked them again. Clean. He smoothed out his pants and crossed his legs.

Aurora emerged wearing an orange halter unitard. She was barefoot and Charles saw that her toes were painted the same nice red of her hands. The unitard stopped just above the ankle, affording him a good look at the unfortunate rose tattoo that started at her instep. He hoped it was her only one.

"I have trouble getting comfortable in a dress," she said and walked to the bed.

Charles was struck by the beauty of her sweeping quadriceps and the nice separation between hamstring and glute.

"Tell me about the Southern States." Charles watched Aurora lay on the bed. "How did you prepare?"

"Training?"

"No, drugs." He leaned forward.

"Twelve weeks out I started on ten milligrams of Winstrol and seven and a half milligrams Anavar, which worked great. I got really strong and thick fast and I didn't hold much water. At six weeks I switched to Primabolan Acetate, twelve and a half milligrams every other day, with three Clembuteral a day and two Nolvadex at night. Actually, at the end, I got up to four Nolvadex, which got me hard, but I started kind of hallucinating. Anyway, I won and it was the best shape of my life."

Charles said, "You couldn't get near the Nationals with that little stack. You know that?"

"More?"

"A lot more, combined with growth hormone and insulin." He sat back and took a sip of water. "If you're serious."

Aurora got off the bed and picked up her purse. She stood with her back toward Charles, squeezing her gluteus maximus muscles. "Even if I wanted to, I couldn't afford that kind of stuff." She turned and stuffed a piece of sugarless bubble gum into her mouth.

"You'd need a sponsor." He drank more water. "Do you remember May Ward?"

" 'Course," Aurora said, sitting on the bed again. "She had an amazing body. She would have won the Olympia."

"I was May's sponsor."

"You were?"

"I spotted May when she won the Iron Maiden. She was just a middleweight then but I saw immediately what she could be. She had phenomenal genetics. Like yours."

"I'm nothing like May," she said, crossing her legs and rubbing the tattoo with her hand. "She was the best. What happened to her?"

"Lost interest." Charles stood. "I had a lovely evening. It's late and you train early."

"It's not that late." Aurora stood up. "You sure?"

"I'll see you in the morning." He lifted just slightly on his toes and kissed Aurora on the cheek, careful not to touch her with his body. "I'll look forward to it." He turned and opened the door.

"Thank you so much." She followed him to the door.

"My pleasure." Charles walked quickly down the hall.

Aurora Has a Look

Aurora stood in front of the mirror, unsnapped the orange unitard at her neck and pulled it down slowly to her stomach. She loved to look at her breasts; they were perfect. She was glad she'd decided on the implants with the nipple raises, much more sexy and worth the extra money. She liked that full, pouting look. She wet her thumbs and index fingers with her tongue and pulled her nipples to full erection, then took the unitard off and stood in her purple nylon thong in a front relaxed pose with her lats flared, arms held slightly away from the body and flexed, legs pushing and pulling against themselves in painful yet delightful isometrics. It was true, she did have good genetics. Maybe she could stand next to these girls, with help.

Aurora did a quarter turn to the right and stood for a moment admiring her tricep, its horseshoe shape finely etched. God, to live in California. To compete in this arena. It would be like winning the lottery.

She raised up on her left hip, reached both arms forward, clasped hands and pulled them back to her body in a side chest. If she moved here, she'd have her own place. She could get away from her mother. Aurora would have a shot at real success.

She pivoted around and hit a front double bicep with left leg extended, her best shot. Maybe, if she had a sponsor, she could beat these California girls. Charles was skinny and she'd never liked little men. He was pale, his nose long and rootlike, twisted like an old piece of ginger. Aurora hated freckles. But he had nice fingers and that supereducated voice. He was kind of sexy in a rich way. He seemed to know what he was doing. He definitely had money.

She tore off her panties, put her right leg forward, toe pointed, knee turned out, brought both arms up behind her head, blew out all her breath and crunched into an abdominal shot. Her stomach was split down the middle with six symmetrical sections and two nice blue veins. She spun around and did a back double bicep but couldn't see much without a second mirror, so she bent over and looked through her straight, stiff legs at her hamstrings and was excited by the deep separation and muscular clarity that she saw. Aurora felt good. She held her ankles and pulled her head closer, admiring herself and wishing that the judges would allow women to do poses like this.

Aurora Makes a Plan

Aurora sat by the open window of her hotel room. There wasn't any traffic and she thought she could hear the ocean if she held her breath and sat quietly. Amy would love California. They could go to the beach any time. The weather was always nice here. If they could move out of her mother's house, Aurora was sure that she and Amy would grow closer.

Aurora had gotten pregnant with Amy at the end of her junior year of high school. Aurora's mother, Eileen, had been furious but refused to allow Aurora to have an abortion. When Amy was born, Eileen took care of her so that Aurora could finish high school. For those first few years, Eileen was the mother of both girls and Aurora appreciated her help. But now Aurora was an adult. She didn't need a mother. Aurora was a mother and she wanted her daughter back.

Aurora had $217 in her wallet and about $300 credit left on her charge card. If she cut back on food, she could last another week. Hell, she'd stop eating if it came to that. Charles might be the answer. He could change her life.

Aurora found the only outfit she hadn't worn yet, her green-and-purple-striped shorts and matching top. She put on the shorts and pulled the center seam high up into her butt crack so that each cheek was nicely delineated. She put on her top, shoes, and socks, and dropped to the ground for a quick set of a hundred push-ups. It was 7:35. Charles was waiting and she wanted to have a nice little pump when the elevator doors opened. She pulled and twisted her nipples hard so they stuck way out, shut off the light in her hotel room, and headed downstairs.

Venice

Charles sat holding his mint tea and watched Aurora eat the mound of scrambled egg whites with bits of chicken breast and mushrooms. She'd already had a bowl of oatmeal with banana and a cup of coffee with two Equals. She sat hunched over the little table, right hand clutching her fork, left arm cradling her plate. Her hair was pulled into a tight ponytail, her green-and-purple-striped bra-top still damp from sweat. Charles sat quietly, not wanting to interrupt.

"They make the best egg whites here." She took a sip of coffee and smiled at Charles. "You sure you're not hungry?"

"No, I'm fine." Charles straightened in his chair and noticed that the waistband of her matching shorts was also damp with sweat. "You had a wonderful workout."

"Yeah," she said, chewing and swallowing. "I liked having you there. Watching me."

The Abdels, Hernando and Eve, walked past the table dressed in their matching uniforms of black-and-red plaid tights with black mesh tank tops and black patent leather Doc Martens with red shoelaces. They each had a barbwire ring tattooed around their left arms and black hair, his short, hers long and braided down the middle of her back. Eve, as usual, trailed Hernando by a few steps. Hernando gave Aurora a thorough look as he passed and Charles was pleased to note her lack of response.

"Who are they?" Aurora whispered.

"She was a secretary. Hernando found her and turned her into a bodybuilder. She won a couple of shows and he married her. He doesn't allow her to talk in public." Charles leaned in closer to Aurora and giggled. "She won the Orange County Muscle Classic in April and he didn't even place in the top five. He wouldn't let her out of the house for a week and when she did finally show up at the gym she had two black eyes."

Aurora mashed the last bits of egg white and mushroom onto her fork and finished her coffee. "Does she have any other titles?"

Charles paid and guided Aurora out of the restaurant. "Shall we walk on the beach?"

Aurora nodded enthusiastically. "Soft sand is so good for the calves."

Charles took Aurora's large hand in his as they waited for the light. A car, full of young Hispanics, their hair shaved, the sleeves of their white T-shirts rolled up, slowed and honked at Aurora. She raised her right arm in a bicep pose and smiled while still holding on to Charles' hand with her left. The boys waved and hollered, shifted the car into neutral for a moment and revved the engine, then drove on. Charles liked her spunky display.

Charles and Aurora walked the three blocks to the beach. The sun was hot and the traffic heavy with people searching for parking spots. The boardwalk was crowded with signs advertising body piercing, tattoos, hair weaving and scalp treatments. A woman with a massage table offered acupuncture for fifty cents a needle. A young, bald, legless man in a rusty wheelchair held out an empty paper cup and asked passersby for money. There was a dwarf, in tiny shorts and a tank top, sitting on a bench arguing with a tall thin man in a ragged, dirty black suit who had open sores around his mouth. The dwarf lunged for the thin man, strangling him. The man stood and grabbed the dwarf under the arms, pulled him away and threw him. The dwarf landed on his back on the concrete but quickly scrambled to his feet, arms raised in a fighting stance. Charles steered Aurora away from this scene and out onto the beach.

"Tell me about your daughter," he said when they'd reached the firm brown sand near the water. A comfortable breeze blew and cooled Charles after the hot crossing. He was not about to walk in that exhausting soft sand.

Aurora pulled her shorts down a bit, exposing more of her stomach to the sun. "She's twelve. Great kid."

"Who's she staying with?" Charles admired her sharp chin line.

"My mom. They're close." Aurora stopped and took off her shoes.

Charles stood and looked out over the water. A lifeguard boat sped past. "Do you two live with your mother?" he said, trying to sound casual. It worried him. The mother could be a complication.

"Unfortunately. I just can't afford a place. We can't wait to move out." She stood up and resumed their walk, shoes and socks in hand. "I got pregnant in high school. The father was out of there before she was born. He's probably in jail. I hope he's dead. Jerk."

Charles smiled, relieved. "Were you a bodybuilder before you had Amy?"

Aurora shook her head. "I was a little skinny thing. I got

pregnant and gained over seventy-five pounds. Luckily I got this great skin. Not one single stretch mark." She pulled her shorts down a little more and showed Charles the smooth top of her left butt cheek.

"That's lucky," Charles said. He touched her spine briefly with his index finger.

"Started going to a gym and met this guy, Skip DeBilda. Vietnam vet, missing his two front teeth. He lived in his car at the YMCA and started training me for free. I'd get up at five every morning and go meet Skip. Had to bang on the top of his little Honda to wake him up and some mornings, if he was deep asleep, he'd sit up holding a big combat knife. First time I just about died of fright." Aurora spoke quickly and Charles noticed that she'd flushed a nice pink.

"He'd train me for an hour and a half. Hard. Made me cry on forced reps. I'd usually throw up on leg day." Aurora looked at Charles. "It was fantastic. Then I'd go to work. I was so sore, sometimes, I couldn't even lift my daughter. It was so great watching my body change."

"Do you still train with Skip?" Charles said, mildly curious. He felt hot in the sun and wanted to take Aurora inside.

"He got strange. One day he'd say his mama was coming to help him get an apartment and all. He'd be all excited for me to meet her. A couple of days later I asked about her and he said she'd been dead fifteen years. Stuff like that. Plus, you know, I was shaping up real good." Aurora wrinkled her nose. "He started getting interested in me. I switched to a better gym."

They walked on quietly and passed a group of children making castles, large mounds of sand studded with bits of Styrofoam, paper, and glass. One of the younger children came parading up holding a dead seagull by the wing. His mother shrieked, ran up to him and hit it out of his hand.

"I'd love for Amy to live here," Aurora said. "It's so exciting. Beautiful." She stopped and looked at Charles. "I wish I didn't have to go back."

Charles smiled, enjoying her need. "I think I'm burning," he said. "We'd better head back."

Aurora stepped on a delicate white clamshell, smashing it to pieces, and turned to follow.

I Do

It was Saturday morning. Mrs. Johns wasn't working and Charles had organized the living room. He'd spent eighty dollars on Casablanca lilies and tuberoses. He placed a large vase on the table, and the room was thick with their smell. The heavy velvet drapes were drawn, and the dim Tiffany lamps cast a soothing light. Aurora would sit in the gold velvet chair with the thick down cushions. He wanted her to be comfortable. He'd sent a driver to pick her up.

The bell rang and Charles hurried to the door. She wore a floral, cotton/Lycra, tank mini-dress that accentuated the width of her glorious shoulders and her narrow, tight hips. The black, strappy, high-heeled sandals were nice, something he might have chosen.

He smiled. "Please come in."

"This is the kind of house that the governor lives in." Aurora stood in the entry hall and turned slowly. "It's like out of a magazine."

Charles let her look. "Can I offer you anything?" He felt the excitement rising from his loins. "Food? Something to drink?"

"Crystal Light?" she said, looking at him for the first time. "Fruit punch, if you have it."

"I'm sorry, I don't have that. Pellegrino?"

"No. I'm fine." She resumed her inspection. "I can't believe you live here."

"Let's go into the living room." He took her tanned, shapely arm and walked down the short hallway to the double sliding oak doors. Charles put both hands on the brass handles, gave a light push, and the doors slid open.

"What is that smell?" Aurora put her hand to her nose.

Charles turned to her, troubled. "Tuberoses and lilies. Don't you like their fragrance?"

"It's real nice." She smiled. "It was just a little strong when you opened the door."

They entered the room. Aurora quietly continued her inventory. She reached for the mahogany box on the coffee table and as she bent over her dress rode up on her legs, almost exposing her buttocks. The box was the size of a thick phone book, plain and highly polished. "What's in here?"

"Have a look." Charles grinned and watched her closely.

"Eww." She reacted as if something dead or rotten were hidden in the box. Charles walked over and stood next to her.

"They're glass eyes," he said. "That cloudy one is almost a hundred years old. Very rare."

She closed the box and returned it to the table.

Charles took her by the hand. "I'd like you to listen to a tape I've made. It's for you."

"Sure. Is it singing or something?"

"No. You'll see. Come. Sit in this chair," he said, leading her. "The only thing I ask is that you do not speak or in any way interrupt my tape. When it's over we'll talk. Okay?"

"All right."

He fluffed the cushion and helped her settle in, then reached behind the chair and brought out the equipment. He fitted her with professional headphones that completely covered her ears, pushed the Play button on the small tape player, and rushed back to the couch, taking an envelope from under the cushion. He sat down.

The blank, confused look on Aurora's face changed to a smile. She looked at her hands, enjoying his message. This was the beginning, where he told her how much her company had meant to him, what a wonderful woman, what a smart woman and what a phenomenal beauty she was. He waited. Her eyes shot up to his face.

This was the part where he told her that the envelope he held in his hand had a check for $10,000 made out to her. It was hers no matter how she responded to the rest of his message. It was a gift to help her on her way. She started to speak, shocked. Charles held his finger up to his lips and smiled. She sat on her hands, squirming and grinning. Next came the proposal.

She looked at the floor now, concentrating. Focusing on his details. He would provide her with a house, a car of her choosing and a generous monthly allowance that would more than cover her and Amy's needs. He would plan her training program and diet, supply her with all the necessary supplements and decide on her contest schedule. He would make her a champion and she would tend to him. Keep him happy on a daily basis. If, at any time, either one of them was not satisfied, the arrangement would be terminated and Charles would give Aurora another check for $10,000 as severance.

The tape machine snapped off. Aurora wrenched the headphones off, tangling them briefly in her wild hair, and dropped them to the seat beside her. She chewed her bottom lip furiously, staring at Charles, then stood.

"You are . . ." She walked toward him. "You are an angel of God. You are my Savior." She stopped close to the couch and squealed. "I can't believe it, I can't believe it, I can't believe it." She jumped up and down shaking the floor in her high-heeled sandals.

Charles laughed and came to her. "So, do you want to do it?"

"Oh, Charles," she said, taking his hands. "I do. I do, I do, I do." She came closer and kissed him. Charles allowed it, accepting her tongue into his mouth.

Closer

"**Y**ou go ahead and shower." Charles sat on the still-unmade bed in Aurora's hotel room.

"It won't take long." She walked into the small bathroom and pulled off her dress without closing the door. Charles saw her breasts in the medicine cabinet mirror. She bent and pulled down her underwear. He was delighted by the tiny tan line outlining the G-string she usually wore. Aurora turned. Her pubic hair was shaved into a fetching thin stripe. Very sporty and neat. "I'll be right out." She closed the door.

Charles took off his shoes and socks and placed them under the bed. He heard the shower and felt himself stir with excitement. Aurora was soaping herself. He took off his glasses and cleaned them with the corner of the sheet, then put his face to the pillows and sniffed Aurora's smell. The shower shut off. He sat up, alert.

Aurora opened the door and stood, naked, her wet blond hair combed back from her face, slick and sexy. She walked over to Charles and stood in front of him without saying a word. He sat and looked at her for a moment, smelling the soap. He rose from the bed and put his right hand between her legs, wetting his middle finger in her, then sliding it along her slit and resting his fingertip on her pulse, pushing gently as if it was some Rewind button in his mind. She closed her eyes and let him. He stayed still, his finger gently pushing. Aurora opened her eyes and reached for him.

"You'll excuse me for a moment while I use the rest room?" Charles dropped his hand and dodged around her to the bathroom. He closed the door behind him and checked his watch. It was 11:02. He'd make her wait four minutes. He pulled off his T-shirt, took the flimsy damp washcloth from the side of the tub, wet it at the sink and rubbed it on the tiny bar of pink soap, then scrubbed his armpits vigorously. His body was pale, each rib visible along the front of his chest. He had burned slightly on the arms below the T-shirt line and at the neck. Pink but not painful. He took off his pants and white cotton briefs, scrubbed his penis, scrotum and rectum with the cloth, then rinsed it and scrubbed again, removing the soap. The kitty bath excited him further and his long thin penis stood out from his body, arching dramatically to the left like a comma. His pubic hair was sparse and slightly red, his pelvic bones visible and sharp; white legs bony, smooth and nearly hairless. 11:05. He opened the door.

Aurora was in the bed, covers pulled up to her neck. Charles stood in the doorway, eyes on her, penis stubbornly pointing to the left. He climbed in, the cheap roughness of the sheets invigorating. Aurora rolled toward him and attempted to kiss his mouth.

"No, Aurora." He grabbed her head with both hands. "No, no."

She moved away, hurt.

"You just lie back." He smiled warmly and threw off the covers. Aurora obediently lay flat on her back as Charles rose up onto all fours.

After

Aurora pulled on her jean-tights. They were new. Tights dyed to look like acid-washed denim complete with five fake pockets. She adjusted the pseudo-distressed seams so they ran straight down her legs and pulled on her pink poor boy tank top. Her hair had dried bent and funny; she wet it and pulled it into a braid. There were twenty minutes before she had to meet him downstairs. She lay back down on the rumpled, unmade bed.

He had smelled her. He had been on all fours and smelled every part, starting with her feet. Sniffing in little bursts. Two quick intakes of breath, sometimes four, then moving a few inches to the next spot. He worked his way up her legs to her stomach, skipping her crotch, and spent a long time on her armpits. Thank God for the shower. She'd been self-conscious, then amused, then aroused by the tiny bursts of air that tickled her skin. But when he insisted she throw her legs over her head, in the beginning position of a backward somersault, and went to work on her completely exposed rear end with the tip of his nose, she thought she would die. He held and sniffed that least fragrant spot on her body, never once speaking or reassuring her, frantically smelling. He stayed there a long time, sometimes grunting, sometimes forcing the tip of his nose to enter her slightly. Her back ached and she worried her legs would cramp, or else she would faint in humiliation, when finally he rooted his way up to her female parts. She was so grateful that he'd moved on; she almost wept. He gently unfolded her body, spread her legs, kneeled on the floor by the side of the bed and continued, this time using his fingers and his nose. Aurora's gratitude changed to intense and somewhat troubling excitement. He opened and poked and licked and she found herself bucking in pleasure and when finally he entered her it was the only thing she wanted in the world.

Shot

Charles stood by the door and allowed Aurora to explore the posing room. She kicked off her shoes, stepped up onto the platform and smiled, admiring herself from all the different mirrored angles. She pulled her clingy red cotton skirt up to her waist, exposing her leopard print G-string and flexed her legs, first left then right. She turned and examined her splendid rear end, squeezing it tightly, releasing, squeezing again.

"We'll work here," Charles said. He walked into the room, stood by the platform and looked up at Aurora. She was balanced on her toes and watched her taut diamond-shaped calves.

"You can see everything," she said.

"You'll pose every day," Charles said. He felt proud and excited. "I'll photograph you weekly." He held out his hand. Aurora pulled down her skirt and stepped off the platform. They walked to the cabinet and he opened the glass doors.

Aurora leaned in. She read the labels on the bottles, ampules and small boxes of the oral and injectable steroids. "You've got everything."

"When you get back from your trip we'll start on Deca-Durabolin and Primabolan Depo."

Aurora stepped away from the cabinet.

"It's safe." Charles squeezed her tight round ass.

"I know." She met his eyes but didn't return his smile.

"It's a basic combination. You'll like the results." He touched her arm. He was anxious to give her a bath and see how she responded to the new nozzle.

"I hate shots." Aurora sounded a little whiny.

"No you don't." Charles wanted to pull off that cheap red skirt.

"I do." Aurora looked as if she might cry.

Charles found her fear mildly interesting. "Step back up on the platform." He opened the drawer at the base of the cabinet and took out a syringe and two disposable needles.

"What are you doing?" Aurora backed toward the door.

"I'm going to show you something." He took out a brown bottle of B_{12} with a silver metal top, in the middle of which was a round rubber insert. "Get up there. Nothing to worry about."

"We don't need to do this."

"There's nothing to be afraid of." He took her arm firmly and guided her up onto the platform. "Pull your skirt up."

"Please, don't."

"Pull up your skirt." Charles was no longer smiling.

Aurora bunched her skirt at her waist and crossed her arms, hiding her hands in her armpits.

Charles kneeled next to her and placed the bottle and needles on the ground. He separated the paper backing from the clear plastic and took out the syringe. "Very important. One needle to draw. One to shoot. Drawing dulls the needle." He held the syringe in his teeth while he opened one of the needles, then attached it to the syringe. "This is an insulin needle. Subcutaneous. Also for growth hormone." He held it up so she could see. "We use bigger needles for steroids. Intramuscular. None of it hurts." He picked up the B_{12} and inserted the needle, tilting the bottle, pushing up the plunger with his thumb.

"Do we have to?" Aurora said. She crossed her right foot in front of her left.

"See. I've drawn it out." He withdrew the needle. "Fresh needle." He pulled off the used one, put the syringe delicately between his teeth, opened a new one and put it on. "Now I get the air out, though those stories you've heard about bubbles aren't true. No danger." He flicked the syringe with his index finger, pushed the plunger in slowly until a drop of liquid appeared and replaced the sheath.

"It can wait till I come back," Aurora said.

"There's a secret to this." He lay the needle on the wrappers. "First you have to relax. Put all your weight on your right leg."

She shifted over, eyes wide.

"Good." He massaged her left cheek, first with one hand, then two, enjoying the resistance of the thick muscle. "Now I'm going to numb the area." He slapped her cheek with his opened hand, a hard but appropriate spank.

"Stop," Aurora cried and stepped away.

"Don't move," Charles said. "Get back over here. Do you want it to hurt? I can make it hurt. I'll put the dull needle back on it."

Aurora looked horrified. Charles smiled lovingly. He held out his hand and Aurora resumed her position. He softened his voice. "Remember what we're doing here. If I slap the area, you won't feel the injection."

She nodded and blinked back tears.

"I'm going to slap four times, rub the spot with alcohol, give you the shot, then cover the spot with more alcohol."

Aurora nodded again and closed her eyes tightly.

Charles smacked her hard, brown butt. He enjoyed the stinging of his palm. Two hits, three. Her cheek was turning an exquisite hot red, the skin slightly raised. He took a deep breath and slapped as hard as he could. Four. She rocked slightly but kept the leg relaxed. Quickly he swabbed the area with an alcohol-wet cotton ball. He liked the look of the moisture on the fiery skin. He picked up the syringe, pulled the sheath off with his teeth and jabbed the needle into her butt. She tensed.

"Don't move," he yelled.

Aurora clamped her hands over her eyes and bit her lip.

Charles slowly pushed out the B_{12}, staring at the point of entry. "We're almost there," he whispered. "Almost." He released the syringe and let it hang, stuck in her, empty and spent.

"Is it over?" she whined.

"Yes." He pulled out the needle, hesitated a moment to enjoy the pretty red drop of blood, then pressed the cotton to the injection site. "All done."

Big Time

Charles hadn't commented on her crying. He gave her a tissue when she started to sniff, then turned and put away the alcohol, cotton and vial. He threw the used needles into the trash and washed his hands. Aurora stood on the platform, tears running down her face, skirt still up around her waist and watched him. He ignored her and that made her cry harder.

"I'll be downstairs." He dried his hands and walked out, closing the door behind him.

There was a bruise. Aurora rubbed the spot gently and felt a small hot lump. She pulled her skirt down. Charles had said that it was from the vitamin. Steroids and growth hormone wouldn't bruise or make lumps. Charles had also said the shot wouldn't hurt, but it did.

Aurora resisted the impulse to lie on the floor and sob. It was just a shot. She stepped off the platform. They had the same goals. This was what she wanted. Charles was helping her and it was a good thing. She blew her nose, took another tissue and carefully wiped away the black streaks of mascara. This was the big time and it was where she wanted to be. Aurora the winner. A new beginning for her and Amy. She peed, applied more pink lip gloss and went downstairs. Charles smiled when she came into the kitchen. There was a plate of steamed orange roughy waiting for her on the table.

"When you're finished eating, I'll give you a bath." He patted her on the head. "You're going to be a star."

Going Home

Aurora's plan was to go home, pack up and get out fast. They could be back and settled in time for school. There would be very little discussion. Her mother's opinion didn't matter. Aurora was an adult. Amy was *her* daughter.

Amy would adjust. Kids always did. This was a great opportunity for both of them, and anyway, Amy was way too close to her grandmother. It wasn't healthy. California was the answer to all their problems. It was the right decision but Aurora was nervous.

Aurora jammed her sneakers into her suitcase and zipped it shut. She sat on the bed and looked at the phone. The hotel room was empty of her now, soon to become someone else's. Aurora felt like an intruder. She slipped on her red platform shoes, picked up her bags and walked out. Charles would arrive soon to drive her to the airport.

To the Airport

It wasn't a high-quality diamond but it was large, set in platinum and hung on a delicate platinum chain. Charles had put the necklace in a black velvet box and hidden it in the glove compartment. He wanted to have a little something ready in case Aurora had second thoughts.

When Charles drove up, he found Aurora sitting on her suitcase waiting outside the lobby. Her knees were pressed together and she had her hands in her lap, covering her crotch. She wore a sleeveless white cotton blouse and a floral print cotton skirt, short but not tight. Her red platform sandals looked summery and appropriate. Her hair was shiny and straight, parted in the middle, tucked behind her ears. She looked fresh and youthful.

"You're beautiful," Charles said as he got out of the car.

"Don't make fun." She stood and picked up her bag.

"This is how I want you to look from now on." He opened the trunk.

She dropped her suitcase in and turned to face him.

"I'm serious." He took her arm and guided her into the car. "Natural. It's lovely."

Charles got in and started the engine.

"Have you told your mother?" he said.

"No. I'll do it in person." She smoothed her skirt.

"She's picking you up?"

Aurora nodded.

Charles reached over and patted her knee. He slid his hand up the inside of her tight brown thigh and felt her cleft through the thin fabric of her dry panties. Aurora didn't move. Charles watched the road carefully as he steered with one hand and with the other tried to excite some kind of response. He squeezed her gently between his thumb and index finger. Aurora shifted away from him in her seat and crossed her legs. Charles glanced at her blank face, then put his hands on the wheel.

"It'll be fine," he said.

"It's going to be a huge fight."

"You're an adult. It doesn't matter what she thinks." Charles stopped at a red light. "When you get back we'll find a house."

Aurora nodded.

"I've got a realtor," he said brightly. "We'll get several choices. Two bedrooms in a good neighborhood. Maybe a pool?"

Aurora looked at Charles and smiled. "Amy would love that."

"I think we'll do the Nationals in April. Gives us plenty of time."

"Okay." Aurora turned toward him.

"The first cycle will be the most intense. You'll gain a lot of muscle. Very exciting."

"I'll get fat too."

"Not fat. Water. It'll come right off."

"How much?"

"Maybe twenty pounds in six weeks."

Aurora shook her head in disbelief.

"We'll have about six weeks for you to get settled in and then we'll get started."

They drove without talking for a few minutes.

"Did you think about what kind of car you'd like? It could be ready when you get back."

"I don't know."

"How about a little convertible?" he asked.

"That would be amazing."

"Maybe a little Porsche convertible. A 911."

"No way." Aurora was shocked.

"You don't like them?" Charles struggled not to smile.

"Jesus." She turned completely sideways and pulled her feet up onto the seat, affording Charles a perfect view of her clean white cotton panties. "Are you kidding?" She shook her head. "Me drive a Porsche. Amy won't believe it."

Charles thought how nice it would be to shave Aurora's pussy and cover it with tart lemon curd.

"You'd have to decide on a color," he said. "Can you drive a stick shift?"

Aurora was having trouble catching her breath. "Yes, I can." She was wiggling in her seat. "Red?"

"No." He smiled, tolerant. "Don't want to be too obvious."

"White?"

"Perfect. It'll be waiting for you."

Aurora was quiet for a moment. She put her feet back on the floor and smoothed her dress. "You don't have to do that," she said, finally.

"I want to," Charles said.

A Private Moment

Dear May—

I miss you. If you would just call, and let me know that you're okay, I won't ask you to come back.

Things are the same. Mrs. Johns is still sullen and grumpy although she does ask about you from time to time. Seems she did notice. Vouvou is still sleeping in the bed with me. Snoring up a storm. She's fatter now. Lazier. She misses you too.

I wish you would meet me in some city and we could spend a couple of days together.

Somewhere anonymous. I think of you every day and how you touched me. I still love you May.

I've been going to the gym regularly. Riding the bike, lifting some weight. I look the same though. You said you loved the way I looked. Was that true?

Were you happy with me May? Were you bored? Did you think of other men?

I'm enclosing the usual check. Please call or write.

All my love,
Charles

P.S. Could you please send me Hendrik's telephone number and the drug code list. There is a young bodybuilder who I've agreed to help and I need to place a big order.
Thanks May.

TWO

The Good Life

Amy said, "Don't make me go. Let's stay home together and anyway I don't feel well."

"Come here, angel." Aurora finished rubbing in her hand lotion. "You can't afford to miss any more. Sit next to me."

"I miss Grandma." Amy sat in the chair next to her mother. "We could go home and live with her if you apologized. She didn't mean all those things. Please, Mama." She leaned into Aurora's body. "I had friends there. I feel like I'm gonna die here, like I'm gonna explode."

"I know, honey." Aurora looked around the room for her other shoe.

"There's no one to eat lunch with." Amy tore part of her thumbnail off with her teeth. "They say I waddle. Why can't we just go home?"

"You know why. We've been over this." Aurora stopped adjusting her stockings and took Amy's face in her hands. "We have opportunities here."

"They make fun of you too, Mom," she said as she stood and moved away. "They say you're a freak and that you take steroids and you want to be a man. They ask me if you have hair on your chest. They think you have a dick, Mom. . . ."

"Amy."

"What? I have to listen to it every day. They say you have to shave every morning, that you have a man's voice—"

"That's enough. Go get ready for school. Now."

"And Charles is a creepy little mole," she said, louder. "I don't ever want to see him again. I don't care if he pays for this house. He can't come here."

"Amy! Not another word. You go upstairs and get dressed."

Aurora could hear her daughter opening and slamming drawers. She sat very still at the kitchen table and waited. Finally, Amy came stomping back down the stairs in her usual overalls with the baggy T-shirt underneath. Her twelve-year-old stomach stuck out and her short brown brittle hair was stuffed under her baseball cap. Aurora reached out for a hug but Amy walked past her to the door.

Aurora put on her black cashmere overcoat and walked with Amy out to the garage. The top was down on the car, so Aurora tied a scarf around her hair. She smiled at her daughter and tried again to reach for her hand as she pulled out of the drive.

"Honey, let's not fight. I love you so much. You're the most important thing in the world to me. It'll get better here, I promise. Give it time."

"Better for you. I don't care about this stuff. You've ruined my life."

Aurora looked at her hands on the steering wheel and felt her throat tighten. "I just want something better for us."

Amy got out of the car and walked into school. Aurora could see her daughter's body shrinking in on itself as she walked past the groups of kids. No one said hello to Amy. No one smiled at her. Amy entered the front of the school alone and Aurora watched until she was gone.

*   *   *

It was a short drive to Charles' house. She parked on the street at the bottom of the driveway. Charles didn't like her driving up. She left the coat and scarf on the passenger seat and straightened her black fishnet stockings. Charles was right, they did accentuate the definition of her leg muscles. She smoothed out her short black suede skirt and adjusted her black halter top and, in her high heels, she started to climb the long driveway to Charles' front door. As she rounded the first curve she saw a gardener digging up plants. He stopped working and stared as Aurora approached.

"Good morning," she said.

He didn't answer and as she passed she tugged at her skirt. She continued up the hill and did not look back.

Aurora could see Charles through the big kitchen window. He sat finishing his coffee and biscuits, relaxing in his usual spot wearing his dark green Chinese silk robe. Every morning he had coffee with sweet yellow condensed milk and two Gerber teething biscuits. He liked to dunk the baby biscuits in the sugary coffee and suck them dry. He looked up at Aurora and it seemed to take him a moment to focus on her through his thick tortoiseshell glasses. Then he waved and got up to answer the door.

"My beauty," he said as he reached up to hug her.

She kissed him hard on the mouth and then picked him up like a groom carrying a bride and took him into the house, kicking the door shut behind her. He smiled and kicked his little slippered feet.

"Aurora, Aurora, Aurora," he said as he wrapped his arms around her neck and nuzzled her.

She carried his slim body through the entry hall, into the living room and set him down on the red velvet couch. Then she crossed to the large picture windows and closed the long heavy curtains against the harsh morning light.

"My dear, you look splendid. Even better than yesterday."

She came and kneeled on the floor in front of him.

"Shall I start with your feet today, Charles?" she asked.

Early Pickup

Aurora tugged the emergency brake and yanked the keys from the ignition. Amy sat on the lawn by the flagpole, head resting on arms. All the other children had been picked up and Amy sat alone, surrounded by bits of trash and food left behind from school lunches. Aurora threw open the car door and ran as fast as she could in her high heels.

"Amy, I am so sorry."

"Hi, Mom." Amy looked up. Her eyes were puffy and pink, from sleep or crying, and her mouth was smeared with what looked like chocolate ice cream.

"Baby, I promise this will never happen again," Aurora said. "I got caught up."

"It's okay." Amy stood.

Aurora bent and hugged Amy's stiff and unyielding body.

"Let's go home," Aurora said. She picked up Amy's backpack and followed Amy to the car. "Are you hungry? Do you want me to stop?"

"No thanks." Amy climbed into the passenger seat and buckled her seat belt.

"How was school today?" Aurora started the car.

"Fine."

"Any problem with the P.E. teacher?"

"It was okay."

"Any news?"

"Not really."

Aurora drove carefully. Amy looked out the passenger window. At the red light Aurora reached over and patted Amy's left shoulder.

"Honey, I really am sorry. Come on."

"It's okay, Mom." Amy turned farther away and touched the window with her left hand. "I'm not mad."

Aurora pulled the car into the garage and shut off the engine. Amy got out and walked toward the door.

"Amy," Aurora said. It broke her heart to see her daughter so sad.

Amy stopped.

"I'm kind of tired. I think I'll call Charles and cancel dinner tonight. We can stay home together."

"That'd be nice." Amy turned to face her mother.

Aurora rushed over and hugged her daughter. Amy clung to her and Aurora felt relieved. They just needed a little more time together. That's all. She'd call Charles and say that Amy was sick.

Angry Charles

Finally, Mrs. Johns left for the day. Charles hurried upstairs and opened the wall safe that was hidden behind the towels in the bathroom. He took out a key and rushed down to the garage, where he opened one of the large cedar chests. He lifted out the top trays that held all his animal parts. Big strap-on moose hooves, snouts, ears attached to elastic headbands, all neatly arranged according to size and species. Under the trays on the left side of the chest were several pelts, shiny and soft. There were tails of varying widths and thickness, teeth and claws. He had an entire dog skin fitted with loops that he could wear. Pig paraphernalia.

He set the trays on the ground and carefully lifted out the cream-colored body corset and hood, his silkworm costume. He hadn't seen it in years. It was reserved for special occasions. Seeing it made him feel festive. He could hardly wait for Aurora. He'd be wearing it when she arrived, lying on the floor in the entry hall. She'd ring the bell and he would tell her to come in. She'd open the door and there he'd be, lying on the floor, squirming, maybe writhing, and Aurora would step over him in her dangerous shoes and he would beg her not to squash him.

He would have the hidden camera by the door filming so that later he and Aurora could enjoy the episode again and again.

The phone was ringing when he walked back into the house. He was happy to hear Aurora's sweet voice, the fantasy having already begun. But then she told him that Amy wasn't feeling well and she was needed at home.

"You're needed here!" he screamed.

Aurora was quiet.

"Did you hear me?" he yelled into the receiver.

"She's sick," Aurora said quietly. "I can't leave her."

"What's wrong with her?"

"High fever, vomiting, diarrhea."

"I don't like this." He stamped his foot.

"I'm sorry," Aurora said.

Charles put down the phone. He carefully folded his costume on the kitchen table, carried it back out to the garage, put it away and locked the chest. He took the key upstairs and returned it to the safe, then took off his clothes, climbed into his bed and willed himself to go to sleep.

Next Day

Charles wasn't sitting in the window having his breakfast when Aurora walked up the drive at her usual time. She stood at the front door and adjusted her short red-and-white polka dot taffeta circle skirt so that the zipper was straight in the back. She wore her hair in pigtails tied with thick twisted pieces of pink yarn. Charles had insisted she dot her nose and cheeks with brown freckles. She did not look adorable. Aurora knelt down to pull up her white bobby socks, folding them above the saddle shoes. Panties weren't a part of this costume, so she had taken them off in the car and now was careful to bend at the knees. Charles had been very specific about the instructions. She rang the bell and waited. Nothing. She knocked and tried the handle but found the door locked. Charles had said ten. She rang again, then heard footsteps.

Aurora turned her back to the door when she heard the lock slide. She bent over and pulled up her skirt, exposing herself, and when she heard the door open she yelled loudly, "Behold, I am pink and fresh. I have scrubbed all morning to rid myself of the terrible stench." Aurora braced herself, anticipating Charles' next move.

"You must be Aurora," a woman's voice said.

Aurora whirled around and saw Mrs. Johns. She stood thin and brittle in her white nylon maid's uniform, flesh-tone support hose, and white nurse's shoes. Her hair was short and gray and her mouth a wrinkled line, lips hidden in the frown.

"Charles isn't feeling well. He said to tell you it's the same thing Amy had." She started to close the door. "He'll call you when he's ready."

No Luck

Aurora added up the cost of rent, car insurance, clothes for herself and Amy, neuromuscular therapy, chiropractic therapy, massage, a weekly manicure-pedicure, hair appointments, gas, food, supplements and even without the extras she knew that there was no job she could get that could pay for these essentials. Even strippers didn't make enough.

Aurora picked up the phone and dialed. The machine answered: "You've reached the home of C. Worthington. Kindly leave a message." Aurora knew he was sitting next to the machine listening, recording every voice that called.

"Charles, it's Aurora. Please pick up." She paused. "I'm sorry I didn't come over last night. I couldn't leave; she needed me."

Aurora paused again and the machine disconnected. She redialed.

"Look, it won't happen again," she said quickly after the tone. "Just talk to me. Let me make it right."

Aurora waited for Charles to pick up but the machine turned off again. She slammed down the phone and yanked the yarn from her hair as she stormed into her bathroom. "Fucking freak," she mumbled, looking in the mirror, hating Charles. She scrubbed the freckles from her face and pulled her hair back into a bun. Then she changed into black tights and tank top and drove to the gym.

He doesn't own me, she thought, driving fast. She parked the car in front of the gym and pulled her gym bag from the backseat. *If he stops the money I'll get two jobs.* She got out of the car, pressed the auto-alarm button on her key chain and walked into the gym.

Aurora usually trained at one, when she finished with Charles. She saw that there was a whole different group training at eleven. She said a brief hello to Joey, the manager, as she passed the front desk and headed out onto the floor. She paused by the leg extension machines and took a deep breath. She needed to collect herself, to focus. She wasn't going to let Charles or anything else interfere with her workout.

There were more bodybuilders in the gym at this time of day. They stayed together in groups of two or three, talking amongst themselves, moving slowly and separately from the normal people training there. A herd. They were big and proud, a different species. Charles had been very clear with Aurora: he didn't want her socializing at the gym. She knew that's why he kept her busy in the mornings and made her train at such a weird time. She told him that she was stronger first thing, that it was the best time for her to train, but he insisted she be with him. Aurora watched as Jim Mann climbed into the leg press machine. It was loaded with thirteen forty-five-pound plates on either side and five stacked on top of the foot pad. She smiled as he started his reps, grunting and screaming with the bending and straightening of his enormous legs. His big muscular friends stood around him and shouted encouragement: "Come on, man, you're a machine, you're a fucking piston. Pump it out, you motherfucker. LEGS!" Aurora headed for the flat benches.

She nodded as she passed Nadia Sorenson with her new

blond hair extensions, and beautiful Tanya Rush. They were training shoulders and didn't acknowledge Aurora, but she saw in the wall mirror that they stopped and watched her as she passed. She felt a flash of heated excitement, vaguely sexual, and wished she had worn shorts instead of tights.

Aurora put her gym bag on the floor next to the bench and bent over to get her gloves. Someone growled, deep and low, and she turned to see Rico standing behind her.

"Careful. You gonna wake him up, he wrap 'round your leg and then you be stuck." Rico smiled and showed her most of his big white teeth. He was beautiful.

Aurora laughed. "I'll be careful."

Rico touched her cheek and ran a finger across her bottom lip, then winked and walked away. Aurora watched him go as she put her gloves on and then loaded the bar with a couple of forty-fives for her warm-up set. She sat on the bench and just as she started to lie down she looked up at the bicycle loft and saw Charles sitting there, glaring. She jumped off the bench as if she'd been burned and waved enthusiastically at Charles. He did not wave back. She started to walk toward the loft but he shook his head and pointed to the bench. She looked at him questioningly and he pointed more emphatically. Aurora sat back down on the bench.

Rico walked back over to her, laughing out loud, and held out a piece of paper. "Take my number."

Aurora sat frozen on the bench.

"Baby, little man there"—he pointed to Charles—"he don't own you. I'll take care of you right." He tried to hand her the piece of paper and looked up at Charles, smiled and waved with his other hand.

She shook her head.

"You scared? I'm gonna put it in your bag. You'll call me." He put the number in her gym bag, then bent and kissed the top of her head. He waved one more time to Charles and walked away.

Aurora didn't dare look up. She lay back on the bench and did her warm-up set, pumping out fifteen extra reps. She sat up and Charles was gone.

Instructions

Aurora—

I trust Amy is better. Interesting how quickly she recovered and returned to school. I too am better.

I've decided to change your program. You need more time. We will not be doing the Nationals but will wait and do the America in June. Your muscle quality is not what I thought and an extra month is essential. We will start your supplementation program on Monday. I would like you to come at your usual time and I will administer your first injection. Your diet, effective immediately, is as follows:

MEAL 1:
12 egg whites
4 oz. steak

MEAL 2:
½ cup white rice
4 oz. steak

MEAL 3:
¼ head steamed cabbage
½ cup white rice
8 oz. steak

MEAL 4:
2 chicken breasts
2 tablespoons peanut butter

MEAL 5:
8 oz. steak
½ cup white rice

MEAL 6:
16 oz. steamed orange roughy
¼ head steamed cabbage

DRINK A MINIMUM OF ONE GALLON WATER PER DAY

You need a trainer. You're not capable of training to your full potential alone. You are not disciplined and are easily distracted. Frankly I was disgusted by your lack of concentration this morning at the gym. You need to be ridden hard. Hendrik has a lot of experience. You will start with him on Monday at 11:00 and will train six days a week.

I'm troubled by your indolent attitude. Your lackadaisical approach to life. Was I wrong about you? Are you capable of greatness? We shall see.

Kindly refrain from calling me over the weekend. I have other affairs to attend to.

Charles

Saturday Morning Before Breakfast

Charles got out the vegetable dolls. They stood twelve inches tall and had human bodies with fruit or vegetable heads. They were made of cloth with a pliable wire skeleton that allowed Charles to manipulate their positions. Mr. Beet had a purple head with wispy hairlike threads sprouting from his pointy root and was dressed in a matador's costume complete with cape. He stood next to Ms. Pea, who had three little heads sitting in the slit of her pod, all smiling, and was holding a bucket. Ms. Peach had an elaborate floral print dress and matching bonnet and was leaning on Mr. Cucumber, who held a tiny guitar. The dolls had belonged to his mother, and as a child, Charles had been forbidden to touch them. Today he arranged them in pairs; there were sixteen dolls total. Mr. Bell Pepper was always paired with Ms. Radish; Charles liked the idea of the huge green head next to the small red bulb. Tomato with yam. Most of the dolls stood on their own, but stubborn Avocado needed to lean on a pillow for support. Charles put the dolls in a circle around his body, his audience, and lay back naked on his bedroom floor.

"Shhhh," he said. "Keep it down, everyone. I'm trying to get some sleep."

He closed his eyes, grabbed Ms. Corn and stood her on his right leg.

"Ms. Corn. What are you doing?" he whispered.

He walked Ms. Corn up his thigh, keeping his eyes tightly shut.

"Ms. Corn, please."

He rubbed the doll's knobby cob head along the shaft of his penis.

"Ms. Corn, we're being watched. What will Mr. Cantaloupe say?" He picked up the cantaloupe doll and walked it up his left thigh. "Oh no, here he comes."

Charles shoved the corn doll between his legs so that the head was partly hidden underneath his balls, its pointy cob prodding his sphincter. His eyes were still shut. He perched the cantaloupe doll on the head of his now-erect penis. Its feet tickled him.

"You can't hide from me, whore," Cantaloupe said in a deep voice.

"Don't hurt me," Corn said in her squeaky voice.

"Get up here."

Charles took the corn doll and had it stand in his pubic hair; the cantaloupe doll stayed on top of his penis.

"I own you," Cantaloupe said. Charles pushed the doll down so that the little feet straddled and pinched the tip of his penis.

"You're right," Corn said. Charles laid her down and forced her legs around the base of his penis.

"You are nothing without me," Cantaloupe said in an even deeper voice. "Say it!"

"I'm nothing without you."

"I am your master."

"You are."

"Worship me."

Charles brought the corn doll up and stood it next to his

penis. He put the cantaloupe on the other side and squeezed the dolls together with his hands, lacing his fingers. As usual he was wearing a condom so as not to mess the dolls' faces.

"Take it," Charles said in his normal voice, pumping his hips, never opening his eyes. "Let them all watch while you take it."

Saturday Morning After Breakfast

Aurora pulled on her white tank top, black leather pants and matching leather jacket with the zippers, buckles and snaps. She looked in the mirror. It wasn't really that cold outside. She pulled off the pants and put on her jean cutoffs. They were very short and she'd opened the side seams almost to the waistband. Black motorcycle boots and black leather gloves with the fingers cut off. Very sexy.

"Amy," she called, brushing her hair. "You ready, hon?"

Amy didn't answer. Aurora twisted her hair in a loose knot and put on her motorcycle helmet. She strapped the helmet, smiled at herself, grabbed a hand mirror and checked out her reflection from the rear. Then she turned, unsnapped the strap and watched her hair tumble out as she took off the helmet. She walked out of her room and called Amy again. Still no answer.

Amy lay on the floor of her room listening to a CD and reading the liner notes.

"Honey, come on." Aurora turned off the CD player.

"You go," Amy said.

"We're spending the day. Come on."

Amy whined, "Mom."

"It'll be fun."

"Don't you have to go back to the gym or something? Besides, I don't want to die."

Aurora picked up the plate with the scraps of spongy, cold, instant waffle. The plate looked as if it had been licked clean, no sign of syrup. "I've been riding a lot. I'm good now. It's safe."

Amy sighed and stood up. She wore old gray sweatpants and a green T-shirt that hung down to her knees. She had on dirty white sneakers and no socks.

"Let's get you changed," Aurora said.

"No. It's okay."

"Sure? How 'bout your new leather jacket and some jeans? Those little boots like mine?"

"I'm fine."

"At least a clean shirt." Aurora opened the drawer before Amy could stop her. There were seven Milky Way wrappers and a large empty bag of marshmallows stuffed in the back behind the T-shirts. Aurora collected the papers and put them in the trash. Amy stood still, watching her mother.

"You'll wear these jeans and this cute little tank top like mine," Aurora said firmly and without looking Amy in the eye. She laid the clothes on the bed, opened the closet, and forced herself not to comment on the mess. All the nice things she'd bought for her daughter were thrown down like the used tissues she found on the floor in the mornings next to Amy's bed. Aurora grabbed the small black leather jacket with the Harley-Davidson patch on the shoulder and set it on the bed. Then she started to help Amy take off her T-shirt.

"Mother." Amy pushed Aurora's hands away.

"Okay. Hurry." She walked to the door. "Wear the little boots."

*   *   *

The Harley was a replica of a 1958 California Highway Patrol motorcycle. It was black and white with a silver star painted on the gas tank. Aurora first spotted it in a motorcycle magazine back home in Georgia. Then, the second weekend she was in California, she walked into Custom Car Collectors and saw the same motorcycle there on the showroom floor. She'd always pictured herself driving a Harley. Aurora bought it, not even thinking about the cost. It was beautiful and very tough. Luckily, Charles liked the idea of her riding around on a police bike and he happily paid it off for her.

Aurora had a pad put on the back of the Springer seat so that Amy would be comfortable. She bought two police helmets. There were sleeker helmets that were more flattering but they were not as safe. Plus she liked the continuity.

Aurora fastened the chin strap of Amy's helmet and climbed on the Harley. She was a little disappointed with the ease of the electronic ignition. In her dreams she had seen herself kick-starting a monstrous hog. The engine turned over immediately. She motioned for Amy to hop on.

It was good that the engine was so loud, no chance for talking. Amy had been busy pouting and hadn't asked where they were going. Now it was too late. Aurora set out for the Pacific Coast Highway. There was a restaurant she'd heard about thirty-five miles up the coast where surfers hung out. It served fresh fish and faced the water. Maybe even Amy could enjoy herself.

Aurora drove slowly at first and there wasn't much traffic. As Aurora felt Amy's body relax, she sped up and wove her way through the few cars. It was great being in sync with her daughter, their weight shifting together, bodies pressed close with the speed. Amy's grasp felt like a hug. They drove through Malibu and Aurora noticed people staring. People walking down the street stopped, cars sped up to get a second look. Aurora glanced at her tanned tight thigh and then at the road again. She felt happy.

At a red light she yelled back, "You okay?"

"Great. I love it." Amy hugged her tightly.

As they drove out of Malibu the coast opened up. There were fewer houses and the brown mountains looked open and wild. Space. The beaches seemed more natural, too. There were big rocks jutting up out of the surf and broken pebbly shorelines. She preferred these to the man-made beaches of Venice and Santa Monica that were like vast parking lots covered with sand and cigarette butts and filled with the constant danger of broken glass.

They rounded a corner and she saw the big sign that said FRESH FISH. It didn't look like a restaurant, more like a shack with a large front porch filled with picnic tables. There was a big dirt parking lot jammed with cars and on one side, in a neat row, stood about twenty motorcycles. Aurora pulled up and turned off the engine.

"This is so cool, Mom." Amy hugged Aurora's waist again, then climbed off the bike and handed her mother the helmet. "We should live out here." Amy took her mother's hand and walked toward the entrance. They stopped to let a white Mercedes pull into the lot and park next to a yellow van.

It was a fish market. You could pick out your fish and take it home or have them cook it for you there. There were soups and salads, too. Amy ordered clam chowder and a side of French fries. Aurora ordered a large piece of halibut grilled dry. She'd already decided not to begin Charles' terrible diet until Monday. He'd never know. They got diet Cokes and found seats opposite each other at the end of a picnic table. Amy faced the ocean.

"This is what I thought California would look like." Amy took a sip of her drink. "Why don't we live out here?"

"It's too far." Aurora looked at her daughter and smiled.

"From what? It didn't take that long to get here. There's probably gyms and schools out here. Why not?" Amy was getting serious and Aurora wanted a nice day.

"Honey, you're right."

The man who took their orders brought the food to the table instead of calling their number. He smiled at Aurora and touched her shoulder when he said, "Enjoy."

Amy opened her two packages of crackers and crumbled them into the soup, then took a loud slurpy spoonful. "This is the best soup ever."

A woman walked hurriedly past the table. She wore a white nylon maid's uniform with nurse shoes and had very long red hair. The uniform looked out of place in amongst the shorts, swimsuits and jeans and the flowing red hair seemed at odds with the outfit. The woman went inside.

Aurora's fish was moist and delicious. She had to make an effort not to eat too fast. "When we finish, you want to go walk on the beach?" she said.

"Definitely." Amy stuffed five French fries in her mouth, chewed twice, and swallowed. "I'm done."

They held hands when they crossed the highway to the beach. There was a small cove with a big rock reef sticking up in the middle of the bay. They took off their boots, Amy rolled up her jeans, and they headed down toward the water.

"Mama, seals." Amy pointed to the rocks in the ocean and tugged her mother's hand.

Aurora squinted, the sun bright on the water. It just looked like rocks to her. "You sure?"

"Yes. They're moving."

Aurora saw a flipper move and as the sea lion adjusted its weight she could distinguish it from the rock. They walked closer and put their feet in the water. It was stinging cold. Aurora backed up.

"Shoot," Amy said. "I wish I brought a bathing suit. I'd swim out there with those guys. Do people swim with seals?"

"I don't, baby." Aurora kissed her daughter's head. They watched for a while, then walked down the beach. A fresh breeze cooled them. Amy stopped often to examine rocks, pocketing a few.

"You want to go drive around? See what houses look like?" Aurora said when they were close to the end of the beach. Amy nodded. They turned around and started back. As they neared the seal rock, Aurora saw that standing by the highway, next to the outhouses, was the redhead in the nurse's uniform. The woman stood looking out to sea, her hair brought forward, covering most of her face, but still Aurora could see the tortoiseshell glasses and the distinctive dry brown lips.

Aurora stopped, looked down at the sand, and took a deep breath. *Not in front of Amy*, she thought.

"What's wrong, Mom?"

Aurora pulled Amy into a hug. "Not a thing, my love."

They put on their boots and when they started toward the highway Charles rushed into the Porta Potti. Aurora and Amy crossed the street quickly, got on the bike, and drove north, away from the city.

Later That Night

Aurora waited until Amy was asleep. She used the phone in the kitchen. She had written her notes on a napkin. Her message was brief and to the point so that the machine wouldn't cut her off. She stood by the sink and dialed.

He picked up the phone before it rang. "Aurora, I was just about to call you."

"How did—"

"I was too harsh. You have wonderful mass. We could be ready for the Nationals if you really want to."

She glanced at her notes. "Charles, you have no right to follow us."

"I was already at the gym. I wouldn't do that."

"No. I mean—"

"I'm excited about Monday." His voice sounded hoarse now. Aurora waited.

He said, "I can't wait to see you change. Grow. You'll be in all the magazines. Covers."

"Why did you follow us? It scared me."

"You'll get big. Hard. Shredded glutes."

"Charles," Aurora said harshly, "why did you dress up like Mrs. Johns? Why were you spying?"

"I have no idea what you're talking about," Charles said in his cold, educated voice. "Let's not have any more bad feelings. Monday's going to be special. Hendrik will be there. You'll like him."

Aurora looked at her notes.

1. Privacy
2. Right to other friendships
3. Amy
4. No respect, no deal

Charles said, "I have something very special for you. A gift to mark the beginning of your cycle. Our adventure. Sleep well." He hung up the phone.

Another Day for Amy

Amy sat in her room thinking about what would happen if her mother died. They call her into the school office. Pretty Miss Lincoln in her nurse uniform, Mr. Freedman, and nice Mrs. Rose from the cafeteria are all waiting for her. Miss Lincoln and Mrs. Rose hold her hands while Mr. Freedman tells how Aurora has died in a crash. Her motorcycle squashed flat by a big semi in the tunnel that leads to the Pacific Coast Highway. She died instantly. Then Miss Lincoln asks if Amy would like to come live with her. Or they say she can fly home to her grandmother immediately, and since this is such a terrible tragedy, and she is going to suffer so much, Amy doesn't need to go to school anymore. Or, even better, Grandma will be in the office waiting to tell her the sad news. Then she and Grandma will move to Malibu because actually Charles was riding on the back of the motorcycle. He was killed too, although he suffered a great deal when his arms and legs were broken into tiny bits, his body reduced to a lumpy sack of goo. He died when he started coughing up blood and it poured out his nose and ears and finally suffocated him. Charles has left everything he owned to Aurora and Aurora has left it all to Amy and now she is rich.

It was Monday morning and Amy had a fever. She'd been ready to stick the thermometer on the lightbulb but didn't need to. Her throat was sore and her head really hurt. Aurora gave her Tylenol and tea, kissed her and left for Charles' house. Said she couldn't be late. Big day. Had to meet her new trainer.

Fuck you, Mother, Amy thought. The word made her feel in control. *Fuck, fuck, fucking shit.* She got out of her bed and walked downstairs to the kitchen. It was very quiet and the white tile floor felt cool on her bare feet. Amy could see bits of dust floating in the shaft of sunlight from the window by the sink.

There's nothing to fucking eat in this whole fucking shit wad house. She opened the refrigerator and pushed aside the container of disgusting gray turkey balls that her mother ate all day long. Amy hated turkey balls; they stunk up the house every time her mother steamed them, which was every day, along with that garbage-stink cabbage. Steak and rice and fish. Fruit. Milk, orange juice, and boring old eggs. Amy wasn't allowed to cook when she was home alone but who would know? She could do it except she didn't feel like eggs. She opened the freezer and took out an all-juice Popsicle. The vodka bottle sat on the freezer shelf. She grabbed that too.

Her mother drank vodka sometimes at night before bed. It helped her relax, she'd told Amy. She would take a little cup of it to her room along with her huge plastic glass of water.

The clear bottle was frosty and there were melted fingerprints when Amy set it down on the counter. She unwrapped the Popsicle and sucked while scratching the bottle. The snowy frost collected under her fingernail, a pattern of circles and squares that she could make disappear with the warmth of her hand. She bit off the top of the Popsicle, leaned back in the chair, and forced herself to swallow. The pain in her throat brought tears to her eyes and the relief that comes with scratching a deep itch. Amy went to the cupboard for a glass.

She took off the top, stuck her nose inside the bottle, and pulled in the sharp chemical smell. Nasty. She poured a little into the glass, swirled it with her finger, and licked off the drops. Not too bad. Amy took a sip. At first there was no flavor, just the very cold liquid, but then she swallowed and her mouth and throat were filled with a horrible taste that made her grimace and cough. She jammed the Popsicle into her mouth, swabbed it around her cheeks and throat, and put the vodka back in the freezer. Amy grabbed a diet Dr Pepper out of the refrigerator and went back up to her room, leaving the empty glass sitting on the breakfast table.

Aurora's on Her Way

Charles thought the three carat diamond pendant insufficient. Alone, it was a sweet gesture, not a bridge builder. However, the pendant with matching earrings would show deep kindness and love. And if he added a lovely diamond tennis bracelet Aurora should easily slide back into place. He put the jewelry in his trouser pocket and went to answer the door.

She had her blond hair back in a simple ponytail. No makeup, complexion smooth and tanned, cheekbones prominent beneath her thin skin. The gray tights beautifully outlined her legs and pubis. Tank top. He hugged her and breathed in, delighting in her freshness.

"It's so exciting," he said as he led her into the house. "Hendrik's not here yet. Come in and let's get you changed."

"What?"

"A posing suit. He needs to see you." Charles released her hand and raced up the stairs, skipping steps in his rush. "I think the white suit. You're still tan enough and white is so pure."

The lights were on in the posing room and the heater had brought the temperature to a dry 82 degrees. Charles wanted to show Aurora off to her best advantage and if she were cold Hendrik wouldn't be able to see her vascularity. He opened the drawer with the suits, took out the white nylon bikini, handed it to Aurora, and watched while she removed her clothes. "I'm so proud of you," he said when she pulled off her tank top and her nipples stood hard like the little knot on the end of a child's balloon. It made him want to gnaw her, remembering his birthdays, the rubbery taste and the sound of his teeth scraping the wet balloon, chewing and biting and sucking until the balloon popped. "I'll pin your hair up. Sit here."

Aurora sat in the swiveling chair and Charles pumped the foot pedal to raise the seat. He brushed then carefully wound her silky blond hair into a bun, securing it with bobby pins from the drawer. "Now, close your eyes." He removed the necklace from his pocket and fastened it around her neck. "Don't open." He carefully worked the diamond studs into the tight little holes in her earlobes and fixed the bracelet to her wrist. She was stunning. "Look."

She opened her eyes and didn't move for a moment, then grabbed the pendant, jumped out of the chair, and leaned in close to the mirror.

"Three carats." Charles nuzzled her neck. "The earrings are two and a half. Very valuable. Precious."

"Oh my God," Aurora said, still examining herself in the mirror.

"I wanted you to have something to commemorate this day." Charles took her hand and gently guided her up onto the posing platform. "Do a side chest. I want to see how it looks with the jewelry."

Aurora rose up onto her left hip, clasped her hands, and pulled them into her pose. She and Charles studied her physique in the mirror.

"It's all there," Charles said. "Spectacular." The doorbell

rang. "He's here. Do some push-ups. Get a little pump." Charles rushed downstairs to welcome Hendrik.

When Charles opened the door Hendrik dropped his leather briefcase and grabbed him under the arms, lifting him off the ground in a giant bear hug.

"Happy to see you," Hendrik said in his thick German accent.

"Yes. Good to see you too." Charles had trouble breathing. "Put me down."

Hendrik, with his Slavic features and dyed brown hair, his height and build, was a classic Bavarian woodsman type, strong and capable. A redwood of a man. It didn't matter that the body was a product of years of extreme drug abuse; the effect was impressive. He looked like a forty-year-old, although Charles knew he must be in his sixties. His white athletic socks were pulled up to his kneecaps and the tight fitting blue cotton athletic shorts rode up high, above his navel. His snug blue-and-white-striped boat neck T-shirt highlighted his wide chest and massive arms. A large gold crucifix hung around his neck on a thick gold chain. Christ's eyes were made of small rubies; the nails were pinpoint diamonds. He gave Charles one last squeeze and set him down.

"She's upstairs." Charles tucked his crisp white shirt into his trousers and led the way.

Aurora sat hunched on the edge of the posing platform, tight stomach slightly creased just above the navel, legs crossed at the knees in a poetic posture. She was studying her bracelet.

"Aurora, I'd like you to meet Hendrik."

Aurora hopped off the stage and extended her hand.

"Beautiful." Hendrik scooped Aurora up into another bear hug. Charles could see her implants were being squashed against his big chest. Hendrik set her down. "About one fifty-five, ja?"

Charles said, "One fifty-four."

Hendrik nodded. "Turn around. Let me see you."

"Get up on the platform," Charles said, happy.

Aurora smiled and walked up the two steps. She stood in the middle, where the light was the strongest.

"Front double bicep," Charles said.

Aurora shook out her left then right quadriceps, swiveled her hips in a sexy loosening of her joints, brought her hands over head, and pulled them down into a beautiful pose. Charles felt proud.

"Nice short attachments," Hendrik said. "Tiny joints." He studied her. "Turn. Side chest."

Aurora pivoted, rose on her left hip, and pulled her hands in slowly, dramatically into her body.

"The boobies are too big." Hendrik shook his head. "Why these girls buy the big ones? Covers everything."

Charles looked closely. Her implants had never seemed a problem. But now he could see how they did obscure part of the pectoral muscle. "We could have them reduced?" Charles said.

"No." Hendrik walked to the other side of the platform. Aurora was beginning to shake a little from holding the pose so long. "Most judges are idiots. Love the boobies." They watched Aurora. "We must work on posing. Look at her shuddering. No stamina."

Aurora shook harder. There were beads of sweat on her forehead.

"Relax, baby," Hendrik said. "Shake out."

Charles could hear admiration through Hendrik's criticism

but he was afraid that Aurora couldn't. "She's got a full package, don't you think?"

"Ja. She can be great." He paused. "With work."

Aurora stood in a frontal relaxed pose. Charles could see that she tried to control her breathing. "Aurora, when you're ready, show Hendrik your back."

Aurora turned so that her back faced the big mirror. She placed her right leg straight behind her, bent her left, and started to pull her arms into a back double bicep.

"Can't see the glutes," Hendrik said.

Aurora bunched the bikini bottom in the crack of her buttocks and assumed the position.

"I think it's her best shot," Charles said, admiring the Christmas tree shape in her lower back and the hard squareness of her rear end.

"Ja. Good vee. Glutes. Traps." Hendrik walked around the platform. "The calves are small, but we can use Pump n Pose."

Pump n Pose was a new compound. Its inventor refused to list the pharmaceutical components but claimed it was legal and that when administered into small muscle groups it could cause permanent swelling of that muscle. Pump n Pose was advertised in underground bodybuilding magazines. Charles had heard it worked.

Hendrik picked up his briefcase, took out a list, and handed it to Charles.

Six Weeks Only

Testosterone propinate. 50mg (1cc) twice weekly.
Deca-Durabolin. 100mg (1cc) every third day
Primabolan Depo. 1 ampule (100mg) every third day.
Anadrol. 12.5 mg daily.

Four Months
Growth Hormone. 4iu subcutaneous every third day.
Insulin. Humilane R 3iu and Humilane N 3iu every third day.

"Now listen," Hendrik said. "We got to watch the clit with that testosterone."

"I know," Charles said and smiled at Aurora who stood awkwardly, looking down on the two men.

"I mean every single day. If it gets red or swollen too fast, we back off. Understand?" Hendrik looked up at Aurora. She nodded.

"I'll do the checking." Charles smiled reassuringly at Aurora.

"Ja. I bet." Hendrik looked at Aurora. "Little girl, you are going to lose that skinny body for a while. You know?"

Aurora stepped off the platform, easing the posing suit from her butt, and Charles stood next to her giving her reassuring little pats on the shoulder. "I know I'm going to put on some size," she said. "I'll smooth out a little."

"Honey, you're going to blow up like a fat cow. Pork roast." Hendrik giggled. "But"—he held his finger up, pointing toward heaven—"it will work out nicely."

Charles nodded enthusiastically, then walked over to the cupboard, opened it and removed a black Chinese lacquered tray. He had everything arranged on a lace doily: sub-q needles, intramuscular needles, cotton balls with the alcohol and a small glass of water for the Anadrol. He set the tray down on the dressing table.

"I love organization," Hendrik said as he unloaded his case. The steroids came in glass ampules, 100mg each, both in clear and brown glass. The growth hormone and insulins were in bottles with sealed metal tops and rubber septums. Hendrik picked up a syringe.

Charles grabbed his arm. "I do the injections."

Hendrik backed away, hands raised.

"Darling, step back up on the platform." Charles pulled open the paper-wrapped syringe and carefully attached the longer, thicker, intramuscular needle. He snapped the necks of the ampules and filled the syringe with the testosterone, Deca-Durabolin, Primabolan Depo; 3ccs. "Up you go." He patted Aurora's bottom as he followed her up the two steps, then knelt by her side. He held the syringe in his teeth, poured some alcohol onto a cotton ball, and held the cotton with his left hand. Then, with his right, he spanked Aurora hard three times. Aurora had her hands over her eyes.

"What are you doing?" Hendrik said.

"Numbing her."

"So hard. You leave a mark."

"Nonsense." Charles quickly swabbed the reddened area with the alcohol, then jabbed the needle in and started pushing the plunger.

"Wait," Hendrik said. "You have to aspirate."

"Not on intramuscular." Charles left the needle where it was and turned toward Hendrik. "Not in the glute."

"Absolutely. What if you hit a vein? Waste everything."

"In the glute?"

"There are veins. Don't take chances."

Charles sighed, took the syringe in his left hand and with his right gently pulled the plunger back a fraction of an inch. "See. No blood."

"Ja, that's good. Do it every time."

Aurora still had her hands over her eyes. "It hurts."

"Almost over, lovey." Charles pushed the rest of the injection into her body, pulled the needle out—he delighted in the suction-like friction, as if the body did not want to release—and covered the tiny hole with a piece of cotton. "All done. Now for the growth."

Aurora peeked out between her fingers but did not move.

"I do this one," Hendrik said, running his hands through his hair.

"No." Charles walked back to the tray, grabbed the skinny subcutaneous syringe and attached the needle. He drew out the growth and both insulins, then changed the needle so it would be sharp. "Lie on your back for this one," he said sweetly as he walked back up onto the platform. Hendrik followed and stood watching as Charles knelt down next to Aurora's body, her hands again covering her eyes, her posing suit riding high above her lovely hipbones. Charles pinched the skin next to the navel and pulled it away from the muscle. "Skin's paper thin." He turned and smiled at Hendrik. "Now, this isn't going to hurt. But it stings a little."

"No. Doesn't sting. Feels cold," Hendrik said.

Charles ignored Hendrik, cleaned the skin and slipped the needle under the skin.

Aurora moaned. She crossed her legs and twisted her feet together.

"Quite a baby we have here," Hendrik said and nudged Aurora's feet with his black leather sneaker.

"All done," Charles said cheerfully, rubbing the cotton ball on her stomach, staunching the tiny drops of blood. "Now sit up, love, and take your Anadrol."

"Ja. Then we got to go build some muscles."

Getting to Know You

Aurora followed Hendrik across the parking lot to the gym. She was sure that he wore a toupee. No one had hair like that, parted so low on the side and lying so thick across the top of his head. It was an unnatural shade of brown that didn't match the hair around his ears. It looked ridiculous. His white legs appeared to be naturally hairless. They were thick and well-defined, mature muscle, but somehow doughy. Aurora thought they would look much better tanned or covered up. He had his ugly shorts pulled up high so that the seam rode up the crack of his rather flat butt. And kneesocks on a grown man? *What has Charles done?* she thought.

"Hey, Joey baby," Hendrik said in his loud "Arnold" voice when he walked in the door.

Aurora held back, pretending to be alone.

Joey looked up and yelled Hendrik's name. He rushed around the front desk and hugged the big man. "Dude." They shook hands and looked into each other's eyes. "When'd you get out?"

"About six months ago."

Aurora moved in closer to hear the conversation.

"Where you been?" Joey said.

"Germany. Charles brought me out." He gestured with his head toward Aurora.

Aurora smiled at Joey.

"Hey, Aurora." Joey briefly acknowledged her, then turned back to Hendrik. "You got a place to stay?"

"Ja. Nice one," Hendrik said. They were still holding hands. "Listen, I got to train her. When I finish, we talk."

Joey pulled him in for one last hug, then released him. "I'm really glad you're back. We'll get something to eat?"

Hendrik nodded, then signaled with his head that Aurora was to follow him out onto the gym floor.

She tried to catch up to Hendrik but he kept speeding up, maintaining his five-pace lead, and so she followed. People stopped him, hugged him and shook his hand. "Ja, ja, we talk later," he kept saying, never acknowledging Aurora. He led her into the second room, where the back equipment was, and set his big gym bag down by the chin bar.

"For next six weeks we concentrate on basic strength exercises." He pulled a leather harness from his bag. It was designed to go around the waist and had a chain that hung down between the legs, where forty-five-pound plates could be attached. "For today you do chins alone. At end of cycle, we will be able to strap on lots of plates." He dropped the harness into the bag and giggled, a startling, high-pitched, girlish sound.

Aurora took out her black leather weight lifting gloves. Hendrik shook his head. "Sissy gloves. You need calluses." Aurora bit her lip and put the gloves away.

"So." Hendrik crossed his arms. "Show me what you can do."

Aurora took a deep breath, jumped up, grabbed the bar and adjusted her hands so that they were about three feet apart.

"Wide grip," Hendrik said.

Aurora struggled to open her hands even wider. She knew,

with her hands spread so far, that she wouldn't have as much strength. She closed her eyes, took a deep breath, opened her eyes, looked in the mirror and pulled her body up into the first chin. It was tight and perfect, head back, elbows pulling behind, chest touching the bar at the top of the movement.

"Nice," Hendrik said. "Thirty like that."

Aurora closed her eyes and focused. At rep six, her chest didn't quite touch the bar and her feet had come undone; at eleven, she only got three quarters of the way up, kicking in her effort, and her arms were quivering.

"Pitiful." Hendrik grabbed her around the waist and helped lift her into a full chin. "We do twenty-five more. Concentrate."

Aurora pulled as hard as she could, her pain turning into anger, and somehow, with his help, finished the thirty-seven repetitions. When she dropped to the ground, her back felt numb, her hands frozen in the shape of the bar. She felt dizzy and her arms hung useless at her side.

"That was warm-up. Come." Hendrik walked away, leaving Aurora to carry her bag and his.

Checking In

Aurora got into her car and dialed the phone. On the seat next to her sat the cooler with her third and fourth meals of the day. She was behind in her eating. She had to eat at least the eight-ounce steak and the rice before she got to Charles' house. He would check. But she was so nauseated from training and so tired she felt she couldn't move.

"Hello." Amy's voice sounded small.

"Angel, I just finished training. I've got to run one errand and then I'll be home. Can I get you anything?" Aurora took a bite of cold steak. It was chewy and hard.

Amy sighed. "How long?"

Aurora swallowed the meat. "An hour and a half."

Amy whined, "Mom."

"I'll try and make it faster. You okay?"

"No."

"I'll be there soon. Take a nap."

Amy hung up the phone.

Aurora started her car.

Less Than an Hour

Aurora lay facedown on the mattress. Her arms and legs were tied with black velvet cords to the four corners of the bed. She was counting; Charles was up to 537 thrusts. On a good day Charles could come after only 300. Once he did it in 211.

"Do you like this?" he yelled.

"Pound me. Punish me." She counted; 542, 543, 544.

"You are tough, like abalone."

"Beat me so that I may become tender." She tried to sound enthusiastic. "And later you eat me."

"No!" He thrust harder, jamming his little pencil dick deeper into her body. "I will grill you with lemon and salt, you sea creature."

She arched her back, raising her pelvis, hoping to quicken his excitement; 572, 573. He was moving faster now, making his high-pitched moaning, the same sound his dog made when begging for food; 583. He started wagging his hips back and forth, burrowing in. Aurora was relieved; it wouldn't be long now.

"No, no, no, no, no, no, no, no, no, no, no, no, NO." He was coming.

He started sucking his fingers and then a section of her hair.

Aurora hated when he sucked and chewed her hair; it got all stiff when it dried.

Finally, Charles stopped and slid his slimy softened penis out. She knew not to ask to be released. He might keep her there all day if she did, so she lay quietly and felt his semen drip from her body and onto the bed.

A Lot on Her Plate

Aurora pulled the car in, turned off the engine, and sat while the door shut behind her. The dark coolness of the garage made her want to slide the seat back and sleep. *Maybe Amy will be napping*, she thought hopefully. She ached from her training as if she had a terrible fever. Once, when she first started, she had trained so hard that she peed blood and got a high temperature. She'd had to go to bed for two days then. This seemed worse. She willed herself to climb out of the car but couldn't summon the strength to take her gym bag. Aurora stumbled as she walked to the kitchen door and worried she might faint. *Something's wrong*, she thought. She walked in and went straight to the phone, steadying herself on the counter, and called Charles.

"I'm sick," she said when he answered. "I feel like I'm going to pass out."

"Have you eaten all your foods?"

"Just the first three."

"Of course you're sick. It's the insulin. Quickly eat some fruit before you go into a coma. No, a tablespoon of sugar. Hurry, I'll wait."

Aurora opened the cupboard, took out the sugar, poured some directly into her mouth and swallowed. She closed her eyes, still holding the counter for support. Within a minute her equilibrium returned. She could breathe.

"Charles," she said into the phone. "I'm better."

"If you don't do this EXACTLY the way I tell you to, you could die. People have."

Aurora was quiet; she felt frightened and weak.

"If you follow our instructions you're perfectly safe. Eat every two hours. DON'T SKIP MEALS."

"Okay." She took a deep breath, her strength returning.

Charles' voice softened. "This is an elite science. Hendrik is the best." He paused. "Do you trust me?"

"Yeah."

"Go eat a couple chicken breasts and some peanut butter. Take a nap."

"Thanks."

"You know, I just might want to see you again today. Call me when you wake up, sweetness."

Aurora hung up the phone, got her food out of the refrigerator, and took it to the table. There was a dirty glass that she put in the sink, then sat down to eat her meal.

Twenty-three Weeks and Counting

Charles watched Aurora slowly climb off the sled of the lying leg press machine and then collapse to the ground as her knees buckled. He could hear Hendrik's deranged high-pitched giggle and saw how he just stood there looking down on the poor, exhausted girl. Her clothing was thoroughly damp with sweat and her face very pale. Charles felt tempted to get off the stationary bike and rush down the stairs to help Aurora but then Hendrik lifted her by the waist and steadied her as they walked to the drinking fountain. Charles smiled. Hendrik was going to build him a champion.

Charles felt proud as Aurora stepped up onto the platform in the same white posing suit from earlier in the week. Her legs were still pumped from the workout and so they appeared full but a little smooth. The rest of her body had responded nicely to her first week with Hendrik. She was still lean but harder and fuller from all the food she had been eating.

"Bravo," Charles said, clapping his hands in delight.

"Ja. She did well." Hendrik stood next to Charles. "Listen, sweetie, turn around. Show us your back."

Aurora turned, put her hands at her waist, and by hunching her shoulders and elbows forward she spread her latissimus dorsi muscles like a pair of beautiful wings. Charles continued his frantic little claps. She released the pose and put her hands on her knees, gently pressing, and showed off her lovely Christmas tree in the small of her back. Then she put her hands over her head and pulled down into the back double bicep and held it without shaking for a full two minutes.

"Practicing?" Hendrik sounded pleased.

"Aurora, would you please show us your abs?" Charles said, his voice cracked with excitement.

Aurora turned and smiled at the men, obviously enjoying herself, then went into a front abdominal crunch. It was all still there, sharp and hard.

"Good. Tomorrow is off. You rest." Hendrik took his keys out of his pocket. "See you Monday."

"I'll be right back," Charles told Aurora, and followed Hendrik down to the front door. "What do you think?"

"She did well. Doesn't complain. She's strong."

"She looks good?"

"Ja. She could be great." Hendrik waved good-bye and walked out to the black Eldorado Cadillac that Charles had rented for him. Charles headed back up the stairs.

When Charles entered the room Aurora stood up on the platform locked in a pose called the crab. It was a pose that only men did as it accentuated the thickness of the trapezius, neck, and shoulders, and even though women's bodybuilding had entered a new and more masculine phase, a thick neck and hugely prominent trapezius were still not thought desirable. Truth be told, Aurora looked absolutely fetching in the position with the tendons in her neck sticking out like delicate bones that could be snapped with the slightest pressure.

"Aurora?" Charles said when she didn't move for several more seconds.

She relaxed and stepped down next to him. "It's a good one for building endurance. Did you see how I didn't shake at all?"

He took her hand and guided it to his waking member. She smiled and gave him a gentle squeeze.

"Wait right there," he said. "I've got a surprise." He rushed down the hall to his room and got the chair. He'd awakened in the middle of the night when the idea struck and searched the house for something that would be suitable. He'd found the perfect piece of furniture in the cane chair from the sunroom. At dawn he took the chair and the serrated knife from the kitchen, the one used for carving roasts, and went to work in his bedroom. It didn't take long; he cut the center out of the chair, leaving just enough cane on the sides so that Aurora would be comfortable. Now he grabbed his creation and a flashlight and hurried back to the posing room.

Aurora had her top off and was examining her nipples in the mirror when Charles came in. She turned and looked at him with interest when he set the chair down in the middle of the room.

"Take off your bottoms," he said.

"I'll shower first."

"No. Take them off and sit on the chair."

Aurora took off her posing suit and walked awkwardly to the chair. She hesitated as she looked at the opened hole in the center. Charles motioned for her to sit and she did. Then he lay on the floor behind her and scooted back so that his head was under Aurora's seat, his shoulders touching the legs of the chair. He turned on the flashlight.

"Comfy?" he said.

"The edges poke."

"I'll have to fix that. Can you manage for now? It won't be long."

"I guess."

Charles put the fingers of his right hand in his mouth to wet them but also to warm them. He wanted this to be a pleasant experience for her.

"All right now, you're going to feel my fingers." He focused the flashlight with his left hand and reached up to begin his examination. As he touched Aurora, she jumped.

"What?" he said.

"It tickles." She settled back down. "I'm okay."

Charles started again and this time she held still. He began at her anus, even though that area was not subject to change, and worked his way forward, spreading and prodding, committing every centimeter to memory. And as he worked he hummed a happy, tuneless little song.

Charles Needs a Change

Aurora waited with her ear pressed to the bedroom door. Mrs. Johns' uniform was far too small. It only zipped halfway up the back, and the short sleeves cut off the circulation in her arms. Luckily the shoes fit. Aurora could hear him moving. It sounded like he was dragging furniture around the room. He stopped and it was quiet. Then she heard the crying sound. He imitated an infant's wail and that was her cue. She opened the door and stepped into his room. Charles had cleared the top of his dresser, moved it into the middle of the room, and covered it with a clean white towel. He lay on top of it, dressed only in a cloth diaper fastened with a large safety pin capped in baby-blue plastic. He looked ridiculous but Aurora knew it would be disastrous if she laughed.

"Is Sweet Boy hungry?" Aurora hurried to his side. "Are you wet?" For one awful moment Aurora thought she smelled shit. It made her gag but she kept smiling. She made her voice cheery. "Poopie diaper?"

Charles stopped his crying and cooed. He kept his lips pulled down over his teeth in an apparent effort to look toothless.

Aurora forced herself to breath through her mouth as she

Katie Arnoldi

pulled Charles' leg up over his head and pulled the edge of the diaper open. It had been only gas.

"You're just wet," she said joyfully.

Charles started to cry again, this time kicking his legs in tantrum. Aurora opened the top drawer of the dresser and took out the extra-large Binky pacifier. Charles cried harder and paddled his arms in rhythm with his legs. Aurora ran the rubber bulb across his lower lip and he quickly latched on to the Binky, sucking furiously. She considered giving him a spanking but Charles generally disapproved of her improvisations.

"Let's get you changed." Aurora unhooked the pin and, with just the tips of her thumb and index fingers, pulled open the urine-drenched cotton diaper. She was surprised to see that Charles had completely shaved his pubic hair. He looked very white except the base of his penis, which was pink and irritated, probably from the razor. She dropped the wet diaper into the diaper pail.

"Diaper rash. No wonder you were crying." Aurora took out the Destine. She had always hated the smell. It was too concentrated, too connected with rashes and the hideous lingering smell of the diaper pail. She'd never used it on Amy. "This will make it better." She smeared a thick glob over the irritated skin and Charles responded by getting hard. He was making happy little grunting noises through his sucking.

"Time to take your temperature." She looked in the drawer and saw that Charles had indeed made his own thermometer. It was a turkey baster, a long thin pointed cylinder topped with a large brown rubber bulb. Charles had carefully written all the temperatures on the side, highlighting 98.6.

"This?" she said to Charles, not quite believing he wanted her to use it. He stopped sucking and nodded.

Aurora took a big scoop of Vaseline out of the oversized

container that sat next to Charles on the changing table, and coated the end of the baster. Then she took Charles' legs back over his head and smeared the Vaseline around his brown, puckered anus. Slowly she worked the baster up into his ass, surprised by how easily and how far it went in without resistance.

"Okay?" She held the thermometer in place.

"More," he said with the pacifier clenched in his teeth. He grabbed his penis with his right hand.

Aurora pushed the baster farther into his body. She had to twist it a little now and then to get past the tough spots. When she had it more than halfway in she stopped again. He hadn't instructed her beforehand and she didn't want to hurt him.

"This good?"

He moaned and nodded. He pulled his penis with both hands now and it looked like they were covered with Vaseline and Destine. "Squeeze the bulb," he demanded.

Aurora hesitated.

"Squeeze it," he insisted.

Aurora squeezed the brown rubber bulb and heard the air explode into his intestines. Then she saw that Charles had come all over his hands.

Aurora wasn't sure what to do next so she waited until his breathing calmed.

"I don't have a temperature. I'm just hungry," Charles whispered to her.

"You don't have a temperature, Sweet Boy." Aurora pulled the thermometer out and lay it on the towel. There were streaks of shit on the sides. "Let's put on a dry diaper and feed you." She cleaned his hands and penis with the Johnson's baby wipes and folded a fresh diaper around his body. Then she picked him up, ripping one of the cuffs on the sleeve of Mrs. Johns' uniform, and carried him over to the chair by the window. She settled into the chair, supporting his head in the crook of her arm and pulled her uniform down, exposing her breasts. Charles started acting fussy again. Aurora held his head with her right hand and with her left she worked her left nipple back and forth across his lips until he latched on and started sucking.

Twenty-one Weeks and Counting

The sun hadn't come up yet but Aurora was forced awake by an urgent need to use the bathroom. Not a painful, stomach flu or food poisoning type need, just the body's insistence on imminent evacuation. She sat on the toilet and emptied herself but was immediately struck by the unnaturally strong fish odor, and when she wiped she found the tissue coated with a foul-smelling orange oil that smeared itself around and resisted cleaning. Aurora tried not to breathe as she wiped at herself in a frantic effort to get clean. She finally stood and looked into the bowl, horrified by the reeking orange oil slick that coated the toilet. She flushed, washed her hands and called Charles.

"There's something wrong with me," she said when he picked up the phone. "This orange stuff is coming out. It stinks."

"Fishy?" he said.

"What is it?" Aurora kept her voice even. She wanted to scream.

"Nothing. It's from the orange roughy. Happens to some people, some kind of prehistoric oil humans can't digest, builds up in the intestines and then comes shooting out. Lucky you weren't training." Charles laughed.

"This happens? You knew?" Aurora couldn't believe Charles would laugh.

"I was at the gym once when it happened to a guy named Vance Milton. He was squatting. Shot out all over his pants. Stunk to high heaven." Charles laughed again. "Was there a lot?"

"Covered the whole surface of the bowl."

"So that was probably all of it. Switch to sole. I'll see you after you train." Charles hung up the phone.

Aurora walked back into the bathroom. It stank like deeply rotten fish and shit. She sprayed the floral room deodorant until the tile floor was damp from the fragrant mist and still she could smell the smell. What if it was her? What if she leaked at the gym? She took a shower and scrubbed her rear with soap. She washed and then washed again, but the smell was in her nose. It was in her body. Finally she turned off the water, got out, and brushed her teeth three times.

The sun still wasn't up yet and the lighting in the bathroom was harsh and unforgiving. Aurora stood naked in front of the mirror and forced herself to look. How had this happened? Five days ago she'd still been able to see her abs, even three days ago, but now they were gone. Now she looked like a normal fat girl with sausage arms and an extra chin. Smooth and watery. She blew out all her air and tensed her stomach muscles in every way she could but the skin just looked thick and loose. No sign of a cut. No definition.

She took a hand mirror from the drawer and with a flash of masochistic pleasure turned to study her ass. The glutes were still high but underneath was a bunch of cheesy-looking crap that she'd never in her life had before. Bumpy, ugly, stored fat. She turned to the side and rose up on her hip, then tapped the fatty area with her hand and watched in horror as it jiggled and shook. She turned again, held the mirror up by her shoulder, and jumped. The legs and ass shook. She jumped again and again, setting her whole backside in motion, then she turned forward, continued to jump and watched as her belly and inner thighs joined the shaking mess that was now her body. Normal people look like this. Disgusted, she put the mirror back and went to get dressed.

A lot of the girls didn't seem embarrassed by the fat. Off season they'd blow up but still wear their skimpy outfits and strut around the gym like goddesses on a catwalk, as if everyone could see the perfect sculpture of their bodies beneath the mold of fat. But Aurora wouldn't dream of letting anyone see her in this kind of shape. She grabbed an oversized sweatshirt and baggy workout pants. Anyway, she'd only gained ten pounds. That wasn't too bad. And what did it matter anyway? If it took a hundred pounds to win, then she'd gain it. She pulled her hair back into a ponytail and went downstairs to prepare her and Amy's food for the day.

Aurora opened the refrigerator and took out twelve hard-boiled eggs and a raw, bloody, three-pound flank steak that would take care of today's and tomorrow's meat requirement. There were still two chicken breasts left from yesterday and a half a head of cold steamed cabbage that she would eat for her third meal. She put the steak on a broiler pan, stuck it the oven, started the water for her rice, then sat at the table and peeled eggs. Aurora hated eggs. She'd found that it was easiest to peel all twelve eggs, throw out the yolks, then eat the rubbery whites as fast as she could. She thought of them as her medicine At first she had microwaved them with a lot of Equal and cinnamon, and it was good, kind of a dessert, but it was hard to cook them evenly and she'd heard that Cory Everson got salmonella from raw egg whites, so now she boiled. Aurora finished peeling, threw out the shells and yolks, turned the steak, got out Amy's Special K with some honey, then went to wake her daughter for school.

When Aurora leaned over and kissed Amy's forehead it seemed to her that Amy pulled back into the pillow and maybe twitched her nose.

"Good morning, Angel." Aurora straightened up, self-conscious about her odor. "Do you smell anything weird?"

"Huh?" Amy didn't seem to be paying attention. She looked sleepy and bored.

"A smell. Kinda fishy?"

"Eww. No." Amy sat up, her voice getting shrill. "I swear I haven't been eating in my room, Mom. Check."

"I didn't mean that." Aurora sat on the edge of the bed and smoothed the covers. "Me. Do I smell weird?"

Amy screwed her face up into a look of real disgust and leaned over to sniff her mother. "I don't smell anything," she said, and pulled away fast.

Aurora stood. "Get up, love. Breakfast's ready."

Day at the Gym

Rico was standing outside the gym when Aurora pulled up. She knew he was watching her, waiting, while she stowed her sunglasses, put on lip gloss, checked her hair and teeth in the mirror, grabbed her gym bag and got out of the car. She felt the heat of his eyes on her sloppy ass as she locked the door. She wanted him to go away. She didn't want to be studied.

"Hi, Rico," she said, trying to get past him without stopping.

He grabbed her arm and pulled her in for a hug, his arms imprisoning her like a straightjacket. His strength and size made it impossible for her to get away. Aurora played dead and waited until he was finished with his little joke.

"Fat chicks turn me on. Can you feel it?" He squeezed her tightly.

She didn't breathe.

"I like you like this, baby," he said. "Big."

"Rico, it's not funny. Let me go, you fuck." Aurora pushed herself away, angry, and he released her.

"Hey, I'm just kidding."

Aurora started into the gym but he grabbed her arm again.

"Stop." His voice was kind now, serious. "What's up?"

"I'm not fat. I'm getting ready for something, okay?"

"No shit." He let go of her. "What show?"

"North American."

"How many weeks?"

"Twenty-one."

"What're you taking?"

"Nothing."

He rolled his eyes. "Please."

"I upped my protein."

"You hang with Charles, you train with the master chemist, you've gained what, fifteen pounds in a couple weeks?"

"Ten."

"Let's see, you must be spending your entire day eating steak. Surprised you have time to train between meals."

Aurora laughed.

"They're gonna take you way up?"

"About twenty pounds."

Rico shook his head. "You ever done this before?" He wasn't flirting now.

"Not like this."

"See, I don't think it's necessary to blow up like that. There's other ways."

Aurora noticed Hendrik's car pull into the parking lot. Rico saw it too. "Your head's gonna play tricks on you. Lotta changes. You should call me." Rico walked away quickly just as Hendrik got out of the car.

Hendrik wore a snug black-and-white-striped tennis shirt tucked into yellow nylon tennis shorts. His kneesocks had two black stripes at the top and matched his black leather sneakers. He smelled strongly of Old Spice.

"How's the little bodybuilder?" He grabbed Aurora in the usual morning hug, smashing her face into his chest, her nose pressing against the large gold barbell that hung around his neck.

He shook her up and down, weighing her. When he set her down she studied the necklace and saw that the tiny forty-five-pound plates on the barbell were rimmed in diamonds.

"You like my jewelry," Hendrik said, pleased. "I design it. There's matching dumbbell earrings. Maybe I give them to you someday. If you win."

"You made them?"

"My hobby." Hendrik handed Aurora his gym bag. "Come. Hamstrings."

Aurora spread her navy blue hand towel over the face area of the lying hamstring machine. The black vinyl was dark where people had laid their sweaty faces; years of other people's germs and stink had stained the equipment. She lay on the machine and watched as Hendrik adjusted the weight stack to fifty pounds. Fifty? She usually started with seventy.

"Something different today," Hendrik said. "We isolate muscle. No more of the cheating with the glutes. Relax." He put his hands on her butt cheeks and shook them. Aurora tensed to stop the shaking.

"Relax."

Aurora did. She hated the feeling of her body being moved, loose and toneless. And what about the fish oil? She felt her face flush with embarrassment, then she forced herself to put it out of her mind and obey Hendrik.

"Good," he said, still shaking. "Like pudding. Now, keep them soft and do exercise."

She pulled the bolster with her heels, keeping her butt relaxed, and could feel the muscle work separately from the rest of her leg. It felt good. She closed her eyes and saw how that leg would look with extraordinary definition, ropey and split. Hendrik had his fingers dug into the sides of her glutes, testing

to make sure she kept them soft. At the sixth repetition the hamstrings started to fatigue and she unintentionally squeezed with
her ass. Hendrik spanked her and she concentrated harder to do
the exercise right. He put his hands on her again and shook while
she struggled through the twelfth rep, the pain in her muscle
traveling to her loins, encouraging her to pull harder and Hendrik's hands there on her butt keeping her cheeks slightly open
so that she wanted to arch into his hands and make that pain
envelop her whole body.

"Good," he said. His hands were gone. "Stretch."

She opened her eyes and slowly climbed off the machine,
disoriented for a second. She put her leg up and pulled her body
over. It felt so good to reverse the process, to open and lengthen
the muscle.

Aurora followed Hendrik through the gym toward the exit. Her
hamstrings were swollen and hot, filled with blood, exhausted.
She loved this feeling, knowing that she'd given everything.
There was nothing left of that muscle.

"So, we have some breakfast?" Hendrik said.

Hendrik never ate with Aurora. Usually he went off with one
or two of his worshipers to the Firehouse restaurant. Aurora
would see him there, sitting in the window holding court, when
she drove past on the way to Charles' house. But today none of
Hendrik's friends were at the gym.

"I've got my food in the car," Aurora said. She was worried
about being late to Charles' house.

"They got steak and rice at Firehouse." He walked out the
front door of the gym and started up the street toward the restaurant, not waiting for her to answer, leaving her to follow
carrying both their gym bags.

Aurora checked her watch. She would be late. She raced to

catch up. "I can't. I gotta go." She put Hendrik's gym bag in his warm, dry hand. "Tomorrow we can eat. I'll let Charles know."

Hendrik continued up the street and Aurora watched, thinking he would surely turn and say something. "See you tomorrow," she yelled. "Thank you." He ignored her and she was angry with him for making her feel guilty. He knew the arrangement, her obligation. She turned back toward her car and breathed out the last trace of Hendrik's cologne.

Words of Wisdom

Charles noticed a light sprinkling of acne on Aurora's shoulders and back as he rubbed the self-tanning cream over her body. They weren't large pimples yet, not angry whiteheads, just small red bumps scattered like freckles on her traps and delts. He didn't think she had noticed yet. She looked smoother now, but much tighter than last week and the female disposition toward fat storage on the thighs and triceps was subsiding. Her big body was galloping toward androgyny. Charles felt delighted.

"I'm proud of you," he said as he nibbled her meaty neck, then ran his tongue up her jugular vein, pushing just enough to feel the pulse.

"How much fatter am I going to get?" Aurora looked miserable as she stood naked in front of the mirror.

"No. You can't think like that." He walked around and stood in front of her. "You are metamorphosing into a magnificent work of art. You are becoming the world's most treasured sculpture." He clasped his hands in prayer. "You will be exquisite."

"I'm a pig." Aurora demonstrated by grabbing a thick handful of skin on her lower lat.

"No more mirrors," Charles said forcefully, walking to the

closet for a robe. "Two more weeks. You'll get much bigger. Then we stop and you're going to drop a lot of water. You won't believe what's underneath. Until then, no more looking." He put the white terry cloth robe around her shoulders and guided her into the hall. He remembered that May had felt this same fear and frustration the first time she got on the serious androgens. It was hard for these girls to see the big picture, hard for them to trust in his supreme pharmacological knowledge.

"I want to show you some pictures." Charles led Aurora down the hallway to his bedroom. He took the three green leather-bound photo albums from the bureau and lay them on the bed. They were embossed with gold writing: "May One," "May Two," "May Three." The pages were rimmed with a tough metallic gold ribbon, custom-made to last a lifetime. Charles handled them carefully. He opened the first book.

"Here she is as a child." Charles smiled. May at fourteen, pudgy and awkward with her crooked pigtails and sloppy clothes, her right hand holding the left arm, smiling, standing in the small yard of her family's house. Even here Charles could recognize her posture, her physical language, and the splendid creature she was to become. "At sixteen." He pointed to her in her cheer-leading uniform, the red-and-white skirt and matching sweater. Those legs starting to form, the perfect genetic sweep of her quad.

"Did you know her as a kid?" Aurora studied the page.

"We didn't meet until she won the Iron Rose." He turned the page. There was skinny May in a bathing suit at twenty standing ankle-deep in the ocean. She had the perfect framework, wide shoulders, tiny waist and hips, and a nice deep cut down the middle of her body separating the two sections of her abdominals. "She had never even touched a weight here." He turned another page.

Nude May at twenty-one, locked in her bedroom with the

camera on a timer. Charles had several pages of these. She looked so sure of herself, so confident in her appeal. The way she presented her apple breasts, one in each hand. Her display of both labial folds, held open by her beautifully manicured hands, were sophisticated beyond her years. And while she was not yet muscled, she already possessed that brilliant instinct for display.

"I'd love to have some pictures of you," Charles said. He put his hand inside Aurora's robe and lightly brushed his fingers over her nipple.

"I don't have anything like this." She pulled away and turned the pages, more roughly than Charles would have liked, until she came to the first contest shots.

"First place in the Novice at the Gold Coast," Charles said. "I think she might have won the open division. Look at her symmetry."

Aurora leaned in and examined the photograph. "Amazing genetics."

"You're easily as gifted." Charles slid his hand back inside the robe, this time pinching and twisting the nipple.

Aurora continued to study May.

He leaned in close and whispered, "Turn the page." Then he ran his tongue around the rim of her ear as she looked at photographs of May's triumph at the Iron Rose.

"You have smaller joints." He untied her robe.

"Your shoulders are broader." He moved and sat behind her on the bed and kissed her neck.

"Your glutes are fuller." He eased the robe off her shoulders and traced the prominent outline of her lower traps with his lips.

"You have shorter bicep insertions." He guided her to the floor so she was kneeling, resting her breasts and arms on the bed.

Aurora turned another page and there was May with her big

trophy at the L.A. "How long between the Iron Rose and the L.A.?"

"Six months." Charles took off his green silk robe and positioned himself behind her, his erect penis resting in the crack of her butt.

Aurora pulled the book closer. "How'd she make those gains so fast?"

"How do you think?" Charles held Aurora by the hips and rubbed himself against her in a gentle humping motion. He reached down and ran his finger along the slit of her swollen, wet, plumlike pussy. "Go on," he said. "Look at the Junior Nationals."

Aurora turned the page and sighed in admiration. Charles worked his fingers in her body and she responded by leaning back against him. He pushed her farther over the bed and entered her slowly. They pumped together through the triumphant pictures of the Nationals and climaxed with May at the Ms. Olympia contest.

Amy Isn't Home Yet

Aurora ran a bath, took off her clothes, and did not look at herself in the mirror before sliding into the hot water. It was two-thirty. Amy wouldn't be home until at least three.

Her body felt sore, each muscle identifying itself according to how many days had passed since training. Her hamstrings were the quietest; they were just beginning to hoard the lactic acid that would make walking such a difficult task tomorrow. This training with Hendrik was different from any she'd done. Her body could usually adjust to a level of intensity after the first week or two. But not with Hendrik. Every time they trained he had new and different exercises that tricked her and left her sore and exhausted. Hendrik was a genius at creating new movements, at hitting a muscle in a way no one else could.

She felt stronger now and her endurance had improved. She knew it would work; look what Charles and Hendrik had done with May. In less than two years they'd made her one of the best. Aurora closed her eyes and relaxed in the water.

Charles had surprised her today. His whispering and his fingers made her actually want to fuck him. She came at the same time he did and with great intensity. Thinking of it brought back a vague throbbing and she considered masturbating. She took the soap and ran it around her nipples so they were slippery and hard; she touched her clit, but couldn't work up the interest. She washed herself instead, scrubbing her skin with the new loofah that Charles had given her.

Hairs grew on her big toes. She'd never noticed that before. There weren't many—four, maybe five—but they were long and a dark enough brown to make them noticeable. At first she thought she'd shave but the hair would just grow back, thicker and more hardy. She climbed out of the tub and got a pair of tweezers from the medicine cabinet, then returned to her bath. She propped her right foot up by the faucet, leaned over, selected a hair, and got a good grip with the needle-nose tweezers and yanked. Aurora could not believe how much it hurt; as if that hair was an integral part of some essential nervous system, the pain shot up her leg. How could that be? It was just a toe. Aurora grabbed her razor and finished the job.

The bathwater got cold. Aurora climbed out, dried herself quickly, and put on clean sweats. As she brushed her hair, the phone rang. It was Eileen, Aurora's mother.

"I just got a letter from Amy," Eileen said, not bothering with a greeting. "She's miserable. Did you know that?"

"She's fine, Mother." Aurora hated to be caught off guard. She gripped the receiver tightly and prepared for battle.

"She's not fine. She's in trouble. Have you done anything?"

Aurora forced herself not to answer.

"Have you spoken to her teachers? Have you gotten to know any of the other mothers? Do you know what goes on at school? Jeanine, have you even noticed her lately?"

"You're out of line, Mother." Aurora cradled the phone between her shoulder and ear and held up both middle fingers, silently telling her mother to fuck off but deriving little strength from the gesture.

"Let that sweet child come home. She'd be fine here and then you can devote yourself to whoring."

Aurora hung the phone up very carefully, before her mother could say another word, then said, "Shove it up your fucking ass till it comes out your mouth. I hate you." She took a deep breath and went back to brushing her hair. Her mother was jealous. She'd always been jealous. She couldn't stand it that Aurora was having success. "I don't need you, Mother." Aurora smiled at herself in the mirror. "We're doing just fine." She walked into the bedroom, lay on the bed, stared at the smooth plaster ceiling.

Aurora woke up to the sound of Amy coming up the stairs. It had begun to get dark. "Hi, sweetie," she said when Amy passed her door.

"Hi, Mom." Amy didn't stop; she continued down the hall toward her room.

Aurora got up and followed. "What's up?" She stood in the doorway and watched as Amy stuffed something into her closet. "What's that?"

"Nothing."

Aurora walked to the closet and opened it. There in the corner was a large green-and-white umbrella. "Where'd that come from?"

"Someone left it on the bus." Amy avoided her eyes.

"You took it?" Aurora didn't want to fight.

Amy nodded.

"Honey, that's stealing. You should have turned it in." Aurora took the umbrella out and examined the wooden handle. "It is an awfully nice one. You don't know who left it?"

Amy shook her head.

"You need an umbrella, huh? You could have used one to-day."

Amy agreed.

"Better turn this in tomorrow, okay? I'll buy you one." Aurora hugged her daughter, then released her and sat on the bed. "How was school?"

"Good." Amy stood awkwardly in front of her mother.

"Sit here, next to me." Aurora patted the bed. "Have a lot of homework tonight?"

"Not really," Amy said. She sat on the bed.

"Want to just forget it and go to a movie?"

Amy looked delighted. "Absolutely."

"Let's go buy a paper and see what's playing." Aurora stood, walked to the door, and Amy followed. "Let's go have some fun."

At Breakfast with Hendrik

Hendrik carefully unfolded his paper napkin and tucked the corner of it into the white collar of his maroon long-sleeved polo shirt, creating a flimsy paper bib. The restaurant was crowded with oversized men and women from the gym crammed into pale green Naugahyde booths. Aurora thought they looked like adults at a child's tea party, squirming around uncomfortably in the too-small furniture, legs bent this way and that in an effort to fit. She and Hendrik had a small table against the wall.

"Arnold worshiped me," Hendrik said. "Wrote me long letters begging for my secrets. Had a picture of me in his wallet."

"No *way*." Aurora said. Hendrik had never mentioned Arnold before. "When was this?"

"Late sixties." Hendrik looked defensive for a moment, but then relaxed. He dumped the bowl filled with raw onions on top of his bloody, rare steak. "Came pleading for help after he lost the Universe and Olympia." Hendrik cut a piece of meat the size of a baby's fist and stuffed it into his mouth.

Aurora opened her eyes wide to show how impressed she was, then cut her small steak into six big chunks and put a teaspoon-sized pile of white rice on each bite. She didn't know Arnold had a mentor. She'd read a lot about his early days— what bodybuilder hadn't—but she'd never seen Hendrik's name.

"I created him." Hendrik chewed with his mouth open and spoke through saliva and bloody steak and onion bits. "He was a baby elephant."

Aurora had her mouth full, so she nodded in admiration.

"They all came to me." He drank his milk and relaxed, stretching his legs out farther so that they pressed against Aurora's. "Sergio, Dave Draper, Franco." He scooped up some onions with his fork and ate them.

"Did you compete too?" Aurora said.

"Of course." Hendrik was annoyed. He sat up straight and pointed to himself. "I started everything."

Aurora waited for him to go on, list his titles, whom he had beat. But Hendrik busied himself with his meal and ignored Aurora completely. The waitress came and he ordered more milk. Aurora took another bite of steak and rice.

Finally he said, "Did you know I created Dianabol?" He folded his arms on his chest in anger. "Ziegler came to me for help, then took all the credit. It was me." Hendrik looked hard at Aurora.

Aurora set her fork down and shook her head. "That's horrible." Why was Hendrik mad at her? She sat still, staring into his eyes, her face blank, trying to show him that there wasn't an ounce of guilt in her. He seemed to be challenging her to a duel and she didn't know why. It was several long seconds before he dropped his eyes back down to his plate and cut another bite. Aurora didn't move in case he wasn't finished talking. Maybe this was some kind of German thing.

Behind Hendrik, the door opened and a man in ragged cut-off Levis, a camouflage T-shirt and filthy white sneakers with no socks walked in. His black-rimmed glasses were crooked on his face and taped at the bridge. Skip DeBilda. He was smiling just enough to show his missing front tooth. Aurora looked down, angling her body toward the wall. How in the world had he gotten to California? She hadn't seen him since the Southern States, when he showed up at prejudging and sat in the audience heckling the other contestants. Aurora had pretended not to know him even though he kept yelling her name, screaming that she was the best and the other girls flabby heifers. She'd been in the middle of her compulsory poses when security forced him to leave. He'd screamed to her, "We did it, Jeanine," all the way up the aisle.

Aurora brought her hair forward over her face.

"And who do you think started the growth hormone?" Hendrik hit the table with his sledgehammer fist, rattling the utensils. "Hmmm?" He pointed at Aurora, waiting for an answer.

She peeked up at him from under her hair curtain. "You?"

"I am the father of this sport." He hit the table with his fist again, a judge with a verdict. "It was me." He was getting loud.

"Jeanine," Skip called. Aurora could tell he was close, maybe five steps away. She kept her head down and held her breath.

"Jeanine Johnson." Skip had his hand on her shoulder. There was nowhere to hide. "I'll be damned."

Aurora remembered his smell. The first time he spotted her on the pull down machine, his arms raised over his head, his body odor brought terrible tears to her eyes like some noxious gas from a chemical spill. His breath in the morning when she woke him up in his car. He wouldn't even stop in the bathroom at the YMCA to brush his teeth or pee. He'd lead her down to the weight room in the basement, in the dark, and train her with sleep in his eyes.

She turned and faced him, remembering how she'd told him,

that night in the parking lot after the Southern States, that she never wanted to see him again. He cried and kept asking her what he'd done wrong. She'd offered him money to go away but he didn't take it.

She tried to stay calm. "What are you doing here?"

"I moved here." He was grinning wide, talking to Hendrik now, too. "Got the old car fixed up and brought her on out." He extended his hand to Hendrik; his nails were packed with black grease and God knows what else. "Skip DeBilda, Jeanine's trainer."

"Go away," Aurora said with quiet hate. "You're not my trainer."

"Was." Skip reached over and grabbed Hendrik's hand, shaking it and smiling with demented joy. "Did it for free." He sniffed wetly and dragged his bare forearm across his running nose. "You ever seen such genetics?" Skip pulled a chair over and sat at the edge of their table, blocking the aisle. "Greatest accomplishment of my life was turning this little ugly duckling into a swan."

"Ja." Hendrik wiped his hand on the napkin. Aurora could see he was annoyed. He pulled off his paper bib and placed his knife and fork neatly on the plate next to his unfinished steak.

"This is great." Skip reached over and pinched her tricep. "You're quite the porker now."

Aurora jerked her arm away. "Stop it."

Skip patted her shoulder. "I'm just kidding." He grabbed her knee. "Glad to see you."

One night, a year into her training, Skip had been teaching Aurora how to pose. The YMCA was closed but he had his own set of keys. He took off his shirt and she had been shocked to see how finely shaped his body was. He pulled himself up into a front double bicep and then had her stand next to him and do the same. At that moment, looking in the mirror at her body and what he'd done with it, his smell changed from bad to good and Aurora got excited and fucked him on the mats of the gym floor. That was the end. He fell in love and became a problem. She joined another gym and told him to stay away or she'd call the police. She managed to avoid him except when he showed up at her contests and made a scene. What an idiot she'd been. That she'd ever touched him, his hand on her now, made the food in her stomach sit uneasy and the taste in her mouth sour and rank.

"Get your hand off me, you piece of shit." The words came out before Aurora could stop them.

"Excuse me." Hendrik put his napkin on his plate and walked away from the table to the bathroom.

The clogged pores on Skip's nose formed a pattern of black dots that looked like newsprint through a magnifying glass. There was white-yellow crust in the corners of his mouth. Aurora took a deep breath. "What do you want?"

"I heard things were going real good for you." Skip reached over, took a piece of Hendrik's steak, and popped it into his mouth. "Always wanted to see California."

Jan, the waitress, came with a tray full of other people's orders: pancakes, chicken breasts, steak, milk and coffee. "You're gonna have to move, hon," she told Skip.

"Sure thing." Skip jumped up, put the chair back, and bowed to the waitress as she passed. "Bet you're training at Gold's," he said to Aurora, and sat in Hendrik's chair.

Aurora bent to pick up her bag. Ignore him.

"Maybe I'll get myself a membership," Skip said.

She signaled Jan for the check. Skip removed Hendrik's napkin from the plate and cut himself another bite of steak.

Aurora stood. She'd wait for the check and Hendrik at the cashier.

"Good seeing you, Jeanine." Skip stayed seated. He smiled and there was crud on his one yellow front tooth. "Bet we'll run into each other again." He laughed as Aurora hurried away from the table.

Intruder in the House

Charles was in his bedroom when he heard the noise, the creaking of a board. He hurried over to the alarm panel by the light switch and the printout read, "Door Ajar, Door Ajar, Door Ajar." Frantically he rushed to his bathroom and grabbed the large red metal flashlight by the toilet. It was eighteen inches long, a good weapon. He tightened the sash of his green silk bathrobe, checked his hair in the mirror and, in his black cashmere socks, crept down the hall to the balcony that overlooked the living room. He peered over the rail. It was quiet. The late afternoon sun cast long dusty shadows. Was that someone behind the curtain? Had someone darted around the corner? He pulled back, crouched down on the floor, and forced himself to take slow deep breaths. It was vital that he stay calm. Charles crawled on all fours to the front stair. Somehow it felt safer close to the ground. He tiptoed down the steps, his heart pounding fast, flashlight in hand. At the base of the stair he braced himself on the banister and poked his head out to look around; all clear in the entry hall. He got to his feet. Maybe this was a false alarm.

Charles slid along the wall to the guest bathroom. He ducked in and stood by the toilet, listening and watching himself listen, in the mirror. There was the sound of doves cooing outside. It was a sound that always made him feel lonely, like that little boy alone on Sunday afternoon with nothing to do and no one to be with. He remembered turning on the old black-and-white TV and watching a horror movie about a man stuck in a monstrous swamp of quicksand and being so scared he couldn't move to turn off the set, frozen there, alone, while his mother took her Sunday afternoon nap.

A car honked in the distance and Charles was about to relax, sure it had been a false alarm, when he heard the creaky door hinge in the butler's pantry and he knew there was definitely someone in his house. On impulse, he raised his flashlight over his head, burst out of hiding and down the hallway of finely polished hardwood floor. It was tricky in his socks but he would not stand for intruders. He slid around the corner, ready to attack, and saw that the swinging door was closed. He knew that the assailant must be hidden within. Charles would wait and assault the scoundrel when he emerged. He stood so that the door would hide his presence and raised the flashlight over his head. He held it with both hands and his robe opened partially. Charles made a quick adjustment, tying the sash in a knot, then resumed the position. He wondered if the force of his blow would be fatal. It thrilled him to think so.

Slowly the door opened and the trespassing rogue stuck his stockinged head out the door.

"Aurora, you didn't wear a ski cap." Charles felt angry. He slapped the flashlight in the palm of his hand. "I can see your ponytail. It's obviously you."

"You didn't say ski cap." Aurora came out of the pantry. Her nose and features were flattened to her face by the nylon stocking. She wore a black turtleneck, black slacks and black sneakers.

"I did." Charles walked away, toward the kitchen. "I said black ski cap." He was very disappointed.

"I'll get one." She followed him down the hall. "We'll start again."

"No, it's ruined." He turned to face her. "We'll have to make do with a massage."

Nineteen Weeks and Counting

Aurora stood, in her too-small posing suit, up on the platform, while Charles and Hendrik examined her. The jiggle and shake were completely gone now. She was simply bloated, her skin pulled fiercely tight, like a dead sow, swollen with water, left to rot in a scum-filled pond. Her skin had a redness to it, like an angry sunburn, the result of her soaring blood pressure. Hendrik had been more careful with her lately, especially after squats. He made her rest longer between sets and encouraged her to put her head between her legs and take deep breaths. He probably worried she would pass out—or, worse, have a heart attack. Often Aurora could hear her own blood pounding through her body and at night that booming pulse would keep her awake.

"She needs more weight," Hendrik said. "We've got to increase calories."

"Forget it." Aurora didn't bother with eye contact. She wasn't interested in Hendrik's face. He was an idiot, a fool.

"Aurora, honey, you can't talk to him like that." Charles tried to take her hand but she pulled away.

Hendrik took out his pocket-sized notebook with the monogrammed *H* on the sterling silver cover and made some notes with the matching pinkie-sized silver pen. "We take her up to four thousand calories for next ten days." He closed the book and put it back into his pocket.

"No." Aurora walked off the platform and over to her clothes. She took off her top, not caring that Hendrik was there in the room to see, and put on her sweatshirt. She hated this body and she hated what they'd done to her. "I feel sick all the time. I'm never hungry. I'm always tired. Forget it." She pulled off her bottoms. She hadn't bothered to shave her bikini area in over a week and the dark, sprouting hairs were poking her skin, causing quite a rash, like a patch of angry redwood splinters.

"What is this?" Hendrik said to Charles.

"She'll be all right," Charles answered him.

Aurora shouted at Hendrik, "No," forgetting about her clothes. "I'm done."

"So this is who you are?" Hendrik walked over to Aurora and stood close, so that she had to smell his onion-tinged breath. "A loser? Can't take it?" He held his fist up in her face. "You waste my time?"

Aurora backed away and quickly pulled on her underpants and sweats. "Look what you've done to me," she said to Hendrik, her voice hard and even. She could kill him now if she had a weapon. "You're turning me into a freak." She looked at Charles. "*NOBODY* else does this."

Charles hurried to her side and put his arm around her shoulder. "No one else has the privilege of working with Hendrik." He gave her a little squeeze and she had a strong urge to rip that small head off its skinny neck and throw it in Hendrik's moronic face. Instead she pulled away. Hendrik stood with his arms crossed, glaring at her with frank hatred.

"There's only ten more days of this cycle." Charles sounded panicked. "I told you this would be the hardest one." He attempted to hug her but Aurora stayed rigid. "You can do this for ten more days."

Hendrik picked up his gym bag. "Forget it. I don't work with losers. Use that smelly trainer from Georgia." He started toward the door.

Charles commanded, "Wait, Hendrik."

Hendrik stopped in the doorway but didn't turn.

Charles put his hands on Aurora's shoulders and looked into her eyes. "If you stop this now your metabolism will be ruined, maybe for the rest of your life. You can't just walk away." He dropped his hands to his sides. "This is a twenty-four week program and you're too far into it now. You can't stop."

Aurora started to cry. She wiped at the tears with her pudgy, swollen fingers and tried to control herself, but soon the sobbing racked her body and she stood shaking in her misery. Hendrik watched her with a smirk.

Hendrik came into the room and got back in her face. "If you ever say no again, that's it." He pointed at her. "You will eat an additional eight ounces of red meat and two more potatoes daily. And keep your scummy friends away from me." Hendrik turned and left.

Aurora sank down to the floor, put her head in her hands, and let herself cry. She heard herself moan and she rocked back and forth. It felt good. The louder she got the more she wanted. Why had she done this? For what? Snot ran from her nose into her mouth and the salty taste encouraged her to explore this misery further. Maybe she would never stop. She could stay in this warm room and cry forever.

After a while, Charles put his hands under her arms and prodded her to stand. She continued her rocking but he wouldn't go away.

"Come on," he said, and pulled her up. "That's enough."

He led her to the sink and Aurora washed her face. Her eyes were even more swollen now, and pink. Her nose looked small with its red-rimmed nostrils. "Charles, admit I look like a pig."

"Nonsense." He handed her a towel. "Remember that, hormonally, you are quite imbalanced." He rubbed her back while she dried her face. "That's why you're having this irrational breakdown. Only ten more days, then we get off all steroids for two whole weeks."

Aurora was calmer now. "What about the growth and the insulin?"

"You'll stay on those until the end. But wait till you see what happens when we stop the androgens." He reached up and kissed her on the forehead. "You're going to love it."

Aurora looked at herself in the mirror. Her chest and face were covered with pimples, her hair looked dull, her skin a dead ugly yellow. This wasn't her. Where was she? She turned to Charles and said, "God, I hope you're right."

Phone Work

Charles sat on his bed with the pictures of Aurora arranged chronologically on the bedspread. There was one for each day of the cycle. In each picture he'd had her stand on the platform in the same pose wearing the same suit. Her elegant body had changed dramatically, just as they'd planned, and Charles was happy with the results right up until this last week. He dialed Hendrik's number.

"Ja," Hendrik answered. There was loud music in the background, a march of some kind with horns and the loud clanging of cymbals.

Charles picked up the most recent picture and looked at it. "I'm worried about Aurora."

"Wait a minute." Hendrik turned down the music. "All right."

"She's jaundiced."

"Ja, the liver is very busy."

"Her eyes are yellow. I think we should cut back."

"Now you?" Hendrik paused. "Maybe you should write her program. I go home."

"She's so toxic. May never looked like this."

"May did." Hendrik sounded angry. "Anyway, there's only ten days left."

"What if there was permanent liver damage?"

"Nonsense." Hendrik's voice was loud and harsh. "Either you trust me or forget it. I'm a busy man."

"Maybe if we increase her water?" Charles didn't want to upset Hendrik.

Hendrik laughed. "Ja. Tell her a gallon and a half a day." He laughed more. "Tell her two."

Charles got off the phone, gathered the pictures, and put them back in the maroon leather photo album entitled "Aurora One." She'd be fine for ten more days. If she started to get sick, they could cut back. Relieved, he picked up the phone to call her.

Eighteen Weeks and Counting

Aurora's voice got hoarse the afternoon she argued with Hendrik. Crying had made her throat scratchy and dry. When she'd gone home from Charles' house she'd made chamomile tea and cheated on her diet by adding honey, but it hadn't helped. Her voice stayed laryngitis-rough for five days and then began to settle into a deeper, more manly version of itself. It cracked its pitch at times like the voice of some pimply adolescent boy on the edge of manhood. Aurora's change had come. Soon people would stop asking if she had a cold and would become accustomed to her new sound.

Aurora stood on the posing platform in her old nylon, stretched-out, zebra G-string underwear and gray sports bra. The posing suits were too small and uncomfortable now. She weighed one hundred seventy-seven. Twenty-three pounds in six weeks. She looked at her feet, her long toenails untrimmed and slightly yellowed, while Charles and Hendrik examined her.

"She held her shape," Charles said. "All that weight and she's still got nice symmetry."

Hendrik spoke directly to Aurora for the first time since their fight. "You did excellent job." All week, at the gym, he'd pointed to machines or weight racks and Aurora did the exercises without speaking. He held up fingers for reps, flashing five fingers three or four times when he wanted high repetition and tapped her shoulder if he wanted her to stop. He walked away when they were finished.

Aurora looked up at Hendrik's face in the mirror. He was smiling wide, the gray-black gum line above his poorly capped teeth obvious and sickening. He wore a beige nylon do-rag that matched his orange-brown Derma-dyed skin, a silver loop earring the size of a quarter from which hung a thimble-sized silver bell that made a soft ringing sound every time he moved his fat head, and a beige and white striped boat neck T-shirt. Hendrik-the-pirate was kissing ass.

"I'm proud of you," Hendrik said.

Aurora felt sticky. Her upper thighs touched and rubbed now when she walked and often she had hot flashes, a result of her hormonal imbalance. She was sweating under her arms and the thin strip of cloth that rode between her butt cheeks felt damp and dirty. Her waist looked shortened and thick, as if the weight of all that muscle on her chest, back and shoulders had compressed her midsection into a stumpy, flesh trunk. Her body resembled a mutant-gnarled and stunted tree.

"Don't you get bored?" she said to Hendrik. "Aren't you tired of looking at my sorry fat ass?" She stepped off the platform and pulled on her grimy black sweatpants and XXL Gold's sweatshirt. She wasn't listening for an answer. She didn't care what they thought.

"She needs a break," Hendrik said to Charles. "A few days away from the gym."

"We'll go to a resort," Charles squealed in delight. He grabbed Aurora's arm. "Agua Pura. Would you like that? We'll leave tonight."

Aurora pulled her arm away and sat in the chair to put on

her shoes. Charles talked about Agua Pura all the time, the wraps and the scrubs and the milk baths. Massages. The grated cucumber and vinegar soaks. Mud stuff.

"I can't." Aurora tied her shoe. Her white sneakers were yellowed and dirty. "There's no one to watch Amy."

"They have a liver detox program." Charles' voice shook with excitement. "Bet you'd drop about six pounds of water."

"Ja. Go." Hendrik patted her softly on the back.

Aurora stood and shook her head.

"You could eat fruit all weekend," Hendrik said. "No protein."

"I can do that at home." She looked in the mirror and made an attempt to smooth her dirty hair. She hadn't had her roots done since she started the drugs and her hair had grown a lot. The blond looked dry and harsh next to her natural brown color. She looked like a slut.

"You can get your hair done," Charles said, hovering. "Facials. Tanning. You'll feel great."

"It sounds good," Aurora admitted. The idea of being cared for made her want to cry. She was tired of being responsible, sick of everything she had to do. It would be great to get away. And Amy was almost thirteen.

"Aren't there baby-sitting agencies?" Hendrik said in a soft voice. He was being too nice and it made Aurora uncomfortable; it was easier to hate him.

"No." Aurora picked up her gym bag. She couldn't leave Amy with a complete stranger. "I'll just relax around the house this weekend."

"I'll do it." Hendrik nodded rapidly, ringing his bell. "Kids love me. Go to spa. Get cleaned out. Amy will be perfectly safe." He bent to pick up his bag as if everything was settled. He turned to Charles. "Stay till Tuesday. Extra time will do her good."

"Done." Charles gave Aurora's tricep a squeeze. "I'll make the arrangements."

Both men left the room. Aurora sat on the step of the posing platform, relieved to have the decision made for her. She deserved this. Amy would be fine for a few days.

Skip

Skip DeBilda sat in his car across the street from Amy's school and watched as she climbed onto the blue public bus. It wasn't safe and Skip couldn't understand why Jeanine allowed it. Kids got taken all the time, especially fine ones like Amy. The bus pulled away from the curb. Skip made a U-turn and followed. He stayed close, didn't let any other car get between him and the bus, and when it stopped to let passengers off he made sure Amy wasn't being dragged off to be raped or killed.

Amy got off at Ocean and Main, crossed with the light, and went into the Duck Blind Liquor Store. Normally, Skip would wait across the street and watch from there but today he pulled into the lot and parked in a space right by the front door. He saw her standing there in front of the candy display, taking her time, memorizing the selection.

Jeanine used to stand like that in front of the anatomy chart at the Y. Every morning she'd study and he'd point out the different muscle groups that, if she worked very hard, she'd be able to see someday. Throughout those first workouts he'd test her. What's the name of this exercise? What muscle does it work? She worked hard and hugged him that morning when he showed her that her cute, pudgy, little-girl legs had hardened and changed and when she flexed the quad just right she could see a little separation in the muscle.

Amy selected four different candies but Skip couldn't make out what kind they were. She paid and as she headed for the door Skip slid way down in his seat. He wasn't ready to meet her just yet. While she waited at the crosswalk, Skip pulled his car out of the lot, drove three blocks to her street, and parked a few houses up from hers. He watched in the rearview mirror until he could see Amy walking safely toward him.

Jeanine was at that skinny fuck's house. She was never home when poor Amy got there and Skip worried about prowlers. Amy was growing little titties—Skip could see them through her T-shirt. She probably had fuzz on her sweet privates. Prowlers went for that stuff. He should check out the house in the afternoon before he went to the school and make sure no one had broken in. The idea made Skip feel calm. He'd be able to relax when she went inside if he'd checked it first.

The best thing would be for him to pick Amy up from school. No more filthy bus. He could move his boxes into the backseat and she'd sit there, right up front with him. They could stop for treats; he'd ease her off candy. She'd tell him about her day and the two of them could just drive and drive.

Jeanine never did get in his car. She didn't like it. That first morning she arrived all fresh and lemon-smelly and tapped so lightly on the window. He loved that timid little sound and he kept his eyes closed so she'd do it some more. She tapped and tapped and called out his name and still he pretended he was sleeping. Then she pounded on the roof and he opened his eyes and she looked scared and shy. The sun wasn't even up yet but she was shining for him.

"Ready?" he'd said, and jumped out, all business. He took a while locking his car so that she wouldn't see his smile.

"Do you need a few minutes?" Jeanine had said. "Shower or something?"

That made Skip want to laugh. She was embarrassed to ask him if he needed to use the bathroom. Such a lady. She didn't know that he got up early, peed in the bushes, and fixed his hair real good so he'd be ready for her. She used to bring him coffee and sometimes the cup would smell like her perfume. He'd keep it with him all day, sniffing her flowery scent mixed with the roasty coffee. He still had those cups in the trunk but they didn't have anything of Jeanine left on them now.

Jeanine had been soft-pudgy when he started training her. Fat from birthing Amy. He peeled her down real quick. He watched now, as Amy got closer to his car. She had the same shape as her mother. Nice big bones. Pretty hands, long fingers. He could peel her too. Maybe Jeanine would like that. Take Amy away and fix her right up.

Two boys around Amy's age came around the corner and walked a little ways up the street behind her. Skip had seen them before. Trouble-boys who rode Amy's bus and haunted the parking lot of the liquor store. Tough kids who spent their time smoking and needling younger kids. Skip had seen them taunt Amy. It made him proud how she ignored them.

Amy was almost to his car. The boys ran now, coming up fast, and Skip could see Amy brace herself. Skip reached under the seat and grabbed the lightweight throwing knives, the sweet ones with the red, blue, and yellow handles. They were small, not too sharp.

The boys were on Amy now. The skinny light-haired one in the camouflage pants and T-shirt that hung to his knees put his arm around Amy's shoulder and said something in her ear while the other kid, dressed all in black with a pimply face and shaved head, grabbed the bag of candy. Amy tried to get the candy back and that made both boys laugh. They played keep-away while Amy rushed back and forth between them.

Skip got out of the car, threw the yellow-handled knife, end over end, and embedded it in the sickly ficus tree that stood growing out of strip of grass next to the sidewalk just to the left of the group. He did it in one graceful movement. Ballet.

The camouflage boy screamed as he released Amy. Both boys stood frozen, staring at the knife. Little boys now.

Skip giggled. He held up the two other knives for the boys to see, one in each hand, then threw the green-handled knife and landed it a quarter inch to the left of the yellow one. Amy tore across the street toward home, her candy left behind.

"Don't run away," Skip said when the boys started to turn. "One knife left and somebody's gonna get cut." He giggled again. The little boys looked so scared now, he wished Amy had stuck around. There was a big pile of runny dog shit next to the tree. Skip walked over, pulled out his knives, and said quietly, "Take off your shoes and socks."

"We were just kidding around," Bald-boy said.

They weren't following instructions, so Skip held out his arm and dragged the knifepoint across the inside of his forearm, cutting himself in a shallow, neat red line. "Take off your shoes and socks."

The boys sat on the sidewalk and pulled off their shoes. Bald-boy had long, broken toenails that were yellowed and dirty. Camo-boy's feet looked soft and pale.

Skip pointed to the shit. "Four parts. One for each sock." He bent over and poked Bald-boy in the back of the neck with the yellow-handled knife. "Hurry."

The boy stood. He looked like he was going to cry. "With my hands?"

Skip was getting bored. "Thirty seconds or I'll get a fucking chain saw from the trunk and cut off your grimy fingers, then you'll have to do it with your mouth." Skip smiled. He liked the idea.

Bald-boy scooped up the oatmeal-like dog dirt and distributed it evenly to the four socks. Camo-boy sat on the sidewalk, hugging his knees to his chest, crying.

When Bald-boy finished, Skip said, "Now, put on your socks and shoes and get lost."

The boys pulled on their socks, tears streaming down their very young faces. Skip could see the brown staining the white cotton tube socks. They stuffed their feet in their shoes, stood, and ran away without tying the laces. Skip looked down the street toward Jeanine's house but there was no sign of Amy. He got in his car, drove to the corner of Main and Marine, parked behind the Dumpster, and waited to see Jeanine drive by on her way home.

Reunion

Amy crouched down small behind the hedge in her driveway. Skip pulled his psycho-knives out of the tree. Poor Bradley. The boys just liked to play around. They would have given the candy back. Skip frightened them. They put on socks filled with dog shit and they cried. Amy smiled a little; it was kind of funny. She watched as they ran up the street, then snuck into the house through the side door.

Skip did not scare Amy. Back in Georgia she pretended she didn't notice him when he started following her after school. He would be there every day, that horrible car wheezing and coughing out smoke. She'd never spoken to him, never told her mother. She thought of Skip as her bodyguard. It had thrilled her when she saw him parked across from the school a couple of weeks ago. A face from home made her feel more settled. She finally had a friend.

Get Away

Aurora bit down hard on the inside of her cheek, again. She could taste blood through the sugarless peppermint Bubble Yum. She had to stop chewing gum; her cheeks were so thick with fat now that they got caught by the back molars. She ran her tongue along the ragged flesh, pushing hard on the fresh wound, and forced herself to pay attention.

"I'll run away if Hendrik stays here," Amy said in a soft, surprisingly adult voice. She stood by the kitchen sink, arms folded across her chest, glaring at her mother. Her hair was longer now, pulled into a ponytail, and her face was thinner, less babyish. "It's an unfair request."

Aurora slumped in her chair. Children were so selfish. She wanted to go get in her bed and close the door on Amy. She wanted to scream. She said quietly, "You just can't let me have anything for myself, can you?"

"Let's not be dramatic, Mother." Amy was calm, her voice soothing.

Aurora started to cry. "I feel terrible. Look at me." She wiped her eyes. "I need time away and you don't even care."

"I do care." Amy came toward her. "I want you to feel better, Mama." She stood by Aurora's chair. "I'll stay here by myself."

Aurora frowned. It was a ridiculous idea.

"I'm almost thirteen." Amy put her hand on Aurora's shoulder and squeezed. "I'm alone all the time. You go. I'm used to it."

Aurora walked out of the kitchen and up to her room without answering. She needed a minute. She felt like grabbing Amy and shaking her hard till it hurt. If she could get away for a couple of days, then maybe she could be a better mother. Aurora knew it was her job to teach Amy, warn her of the dangers of the world. Teach her to defend herself. Demonstrate proper values like discipline, hard work, ambition. Manners. It was Aurora's job to see that Amy had a good opinion of herself. That she did well in school. Nice friends. Proper foods. Sunscreen. Did her homework. Flossed. That she had well-fitting shoes and clean underwear. Nice clothes. Short, tidy fingernails. That she watched appropriate television, no R-rated movies, and be protected from sex and violence in the media. She was supposed to be close to her daughter. Aurora was sick of her job.

She pulled down the quilt, lay under the covers. She could smell herself, still sticky from her workout, but she didn't move. She didn't have the will to take a shower and closed her eyes. Maybe Amy would be all right for a couple of days. There was plenty of food. If she stayed home, didn't go outside, what could happen? Aurora relaxed and was drifting toward sleep when the phone rang.

"I want to speak to Amy," Eileen said.

"You don't say hello to me anymore, Mother?"

"There's no communicating with you. May I speak with MY granddaughter?"

"She's not here." Aurora didn't need her mother's opinion on the weekend plans. "She's playing at a friend's."

"Amy doesn't have any friends. Put her on."

"She's made a friend."

"You're lying. What have you done to that poor child?" Eileen sounded hysterical. "AMY," she yelled into the phone. "AM-MMYYYY!"

"Jesus, Mother." Aurora held the receiver away from her ear. "Hold on."

Aurora set the phone on her bed and went to the top of the stairs to call Amy, then rushed back to her room and listened when her daughter picked up the phone.

"You can hang up now, Jeanine," Eileen said when Amy answered.

Aurora breathed quietly through her mouth. She didn't move.

"Hang up the GOD DAMN PHONE!"

Aurora slammed down the phone and sat for a minute on the edge of her bed. She was breathing hard. She felt like she'd just been sent to her room or grounded for the weekend. She felt like her mother still had the power to take away the things that she wanted the most. God, it pissed her off. How could Eileen control her as if she were still twelve years old? This was Aurora's life; it was her daughter on the phone. She stood up from her bed and stormed down the stairs to the kitchen where Amy was.

Amy had wrapped herself in the extra-long phone cord by turning around and around while talking. She looked like she'd been tied up, one arm flat to her side, the other poking out, holding the receiver to her ear. Aurora hated it when Amy did that; it left the cord all tangled and hard to manage.

"She just came in," Amy said into the receiver. She paused for a moment, then started turning counterclockwise, untying herself. When she was free she handed the phone to Aurora.

"If you leave that child alone I will send the sheriff, so help me God," Eileen said.

"Give me a little fucking credit." Aurora watched Amy walk out of the kitchen and up the stairs.

"You've always been selfish. Even as a little girl you didn't care about anything but yourself. Now you're sacrificing that child for God knows what."

"I'm her mother," Aurora said. "Not you."

"Then start acting like it," Eileen said.

Aurora paused. Her body was electric with anger and guilt; her hands shook. She forced herself to slow her breathing, then calmly said, "I would never leave my daughter alone."

"Please send that sweet child home to me," Eileen pleaded. "She's so unhappy."

"It's getting better here. She'll be fine." Aurora hung up, then walked to the base of the stairs and yelled, "Amy, honey. I've decided to stay home with you this weekend."

Change of Plans

Charles wore his mother's nubby gray wool coatdress with the white linen collar and cuffs and a short, curly light-brown wig. The dress was mid-calf length, and large through the bosom, but fit nicely through the waist and hips. He carefully slipped on thick flesh-colored support hose with a control top panel that was thrillingly snug; unfortunately his mother's shoes were a size too small. Maybe there'd be time to stop and buy some shoes. He applied her brunt-orange shade of lipstick and a modest amount of blush. The gold ball drop-earrings pinched but looked very pretty with the outfit. Charles stood in front of the posing room mirror and admired himself. He was pleased with the maternal resemblance, and though he'd never actually run though the "mother" scenario, he'd been dreaming about it for some time. Aurora was just the right size now to play the angry gardener who hadn't been paid in over a month. It would be a nasty rape scene, possibly bloody. He made a mental note to pack the tube of fake blood. It was going to be a glorious weekend.

Charles took off the dress and was hanging it in the travel bag when the doorbell rang. He went to the intercom.

"I can't go," Aurora sobbed, her loud, hysterical voice distorted through the speaker.

Charles rushed down the stairs wearing the modest white nylon slip, brassiere, panty hose, wig and earrings. He pulled open the door and saw Aurora sitting in a ball on the doormat crying into her hands. She was in the same sweatpants and shirt from earlier in the day. Her dirty hair sectioned and fell in her face; it needed to be cut and colored. In his gentlest voice Charles called her name. She didn't look up but cried harder, rocking back and forth. All this crying was getting tiresome. He said her name again with authority.

Aurora slowly, and in Charles' opinion far too dramatically, raised her head, wiped her eyes and looked up at him.

"Why are you dressed like that?" she asked, not crying.

"I was packing." Charles helped her up, brought her inside, and by the time he'd closed the front door Aurora was sobbing again. "What's happened?" He tried to sound sympathetic but really her emotional outbreaks were irritating.

She threw her thick arms around his neck, hunched over, and buried her face in his shoulder. Charles steadied himself under her weight. She smelled like the crusty sweat in dank dark privates and men's shoes and bile mixed with the bitterness of her protein-chemical secretions. Aurora needed a shower.

"The boils on my back won't heal. They bleed on my clothes." She sniffed. "Amy's gonna run away. My mother's gonna call the police."

Charles felt the hot slime of Aurora's tears and mucus on his shoulder. He eased her off his body and guided her into the kitchen. As they walked past the counter she grabbed a paper towel and blew her nose, then wiped her face with the soiled towel. When she was seated at the breakfast table Charles said, "Let me see the boil."

Aurora pulled off her sweatshirt. The elastic on the sides of the gray bra had broken; little white threads stuck out through the fabric where Aurora's flesh strained through. Her back was covered with pimples and there were two quarter-sized boils, one near her right shoulder and the other at the base of her neck. Both were caked with blood.

"You've been picking," Charles said matter-of-factly.

"NO," Aurora wailed. "I leave them alone like you said. They still bleed." She put her head down on the table; her body heaved with her cries.

Charles lost his temper. "Grow up." He walked into the butler's pantry and got the first aid kit. "Your skin will clear up." He stepped behind her chair. "Your weight will go down." He swabbed the boil on her neck with alcohol. Aurora flinched but kept her head down. "You're right on schedule and frankly I'm tired of all this whining." Charles lanced the boil with a scalpel and squeezed a pea-sized bulb of pus from the bloody sore.

Aurora body shook with more crying but she kept quiet. Charles lanced the other one, cleaned them with alcohol again, applied antibiotic ointment and covered them with bandages. "Shower more often. You need to keep your skin clean so you don't get these little infections." He threw the bloody cotton balls into the trash and washed his hands. "What else?"

"I'm a terrible mother," she wailed without lifting her head.

"Nonsense," Charles said. "The child is well provided for." It annoyed him that Aurora made no effort to control herself.

"I need to spend time with her." Aurora looked up from the table. Her face was red, blotchy, and shiny with thick snail-track mucus and tears. "Amy needs a mother."

Charles brought a box of tissues to the table. He didn't want to sit down; this kind of self-indulgence was repellent. "You and Amy go to Agua Pura," he said. "Get this taken care of."

"What about you?" Aurora looked more pleased than concerned. It annoyed Charles.

"I'll make other plans," he said. "But no more of this nonsense when you get back. You've got to focus on the next sixteen weeks. Understand?"

Aurora got up from the chair and barreled toward him for another hug. Charles stopped her by grabbing her shoulders. "You'll pull yourself together?"

She nodded obediently.

Charles patted her on the head and showed her to the door.

Something New

Charles went upstairs and took off his mother's slip, earrings, and makeup. He went to his bedroom and arranged the six pillows on his bed into a big down-nest, then crawled in and took out the magazine.

It was called *Delux* and was a catalog of women. It had a female bodybuilder on the cover in a conventional black posing suit, flexing on an apparent stage in front of a car-sized orange-sunset backdrop. Inside, each girl had two pages, one with competition pictures and statistics such as age, height, weight, and titles. The other page was more personalized, with photos of the girls in casual positions, some with a paragraph outlining their special interests. Most of the girls opted for lingerie or hard leather-wear as their signature outfit, though some were topless and a few nude. Every one of them wore high heels. There was a toll-free number on the bottom of the pages with a note encouraging readers to call and place an order today. Exactly what services were offered and costs were not discussed in print. This was the first edition of Hendrik's creation, and he had dropped it off to Charles earlier that afternoon.

Charles had refused to invest in the project and it had caused some hard feelings. He didn't think that there would be many girls willing to participate. He wasn't sure there'd be a market. Now, looking at the finished product, he had to admit that Hendrik had done a beautiful job. This was a very slick publication; thick glossy paper and crisp photographs made it look like a *Cosmo* or *Vogue*. And the quality of women was outstanding, big beautiful girls, some of them quite well known.

Charles felt himself stir with hot blood as he opened to the first page and gazed upon Angel Ray on a stairway, straddling a carved mahogany banister. The stained-glass windows in the background gave the feeling of a church or a grand library—a sacred place. Angel was wearing a leopard-print scarf tied across her chest. She was smiling, bent over the rail as if she was going to slide down, holding tight so that her splendid arms popped with ropey muscle. She appeared to be bottomless, but it was a side shot so only her right glut showed. Angel was the grand dame of the sport, a four-time Ms. Olympia in the early eighties; she was now retired from bodybuilding and pursuing an acting career. Her body still looked fabulous. Charles was shocked and delighted to see her in Hendrik's magazine.

There were many variations on leather, strappy suits with buckles and hooks, jumpsuits with strategic peek-a-boo holes. Julie Holmes wore a black leather thong and a chain bra, woven like a spiderweb over her bosoms, the center of the web open in a round hole that allowed her erect nipples to poke forth. Charles studied this photograph, fascinated by the links of the chain and how they pinched at the sides of her very tanned breasts. He took a paper clip from the bedside table and marked the page.

Cookie Lazar's page was excellent. She stood in a twisting pose, back end to the camera, wearing black leather chaps, her full-dynamic buttocks beautifully highlighted. She held a long piece of three-inch-thick black rope over her head and it coiled artistically on each side of her body at her feet. Her strength and confidence were evident in her tense and serious gaze. Charles marked this page as well.

Ladair Simms wore a pink transparent baby-doll nightie and matching pink heels. She had herself handcuffed to a wrought iron gate, arms above her head and spread wide, in what looked like someone's driveway. Her face spoke of pain. Charles saw Ladair at the gym almost daily. He'd always thought her rather dull. He giggled and marked the page.

Kim Elway and Andrea Star shared four pages with a series of pictures showing the girls wrestling in the nude. Charles put a paper clip on them as well as the page of Doughdee Gates. She looked impressive in her competition shots. She was black, six feet tall and competed at two hundred pounds, but what caught his attention was her personal page where she stood in a white posing suit holding a bull skull, complete with horns, over her head, obscuring her face.

Charles dialed the toll-free number.

Hendrik answered on the first ring, "Deluxe. We're here to serve you."

"Why are you answering?" Charles said. "It's horrible. You need a woman."

"Ja?" Hendrik said. "Who's going to pay for woman?"

"You ruin the mood."

"When I make money, I buy woman. Okay?"

"What about when you're not there?"

"Answering machine. I call back. Start over." Hendrik cleared his throat. "Deluxe. We're here to serve."

"Just say 'Deluxe.' It's better."

Hendrik paused and then, a little impatiently, said, "Deluxe."

"Yes." Charles snuggled down in his pillows, enjoying his role. "I'm calling to inquire about your magazine. I'd like to order something."

"Give me page number."

"NO," Charles said. "You say, 'Certainly. May I have the page number?' "

"Okay." Hendrik sounded mad. "Go on."

"There's several," Charles said. "The first is page two, Angel Ray."

"Good choice. Angel is an ex–Miss Olympia as well as a certified masseuse. She will come to your house for two hundred dollars an hour, two-hour minimum, and brings with her an assortment of outfits in which she will pose while rubbing your body."

"Perfect, Hendrik," Charles said. "On page thirty-two, Cookie Lazar."

"Ja. Cookie is an expert wrangler. She does amazing tricks with both nylon and velvet rope. She is an enthusiastic lesbian and works well in groups but also enjoys our male clientele. Very versatile. She charges a hundred dollars an hour with the two-hour minimum."

"Page sixty-seven."

"Ah, the girls. Very popular. They are both regional champions. Kim was Ms. Orange County and Andrea Ms. Palm Springs. They work together and will come to your house. They tie you to your chair or bed, whatever you prefer, and then wrestle for approximately an hour and a half. Usually nude, although they have an extensive costume wardrobe for the customer to choose from. The cost is five hundred dollars and they will either leave you bound when the show is over or untie you when they leave. Again, it's whatever you choose."

"I can't wrestle with them?"

"Absolutely not."

"That's kind of expensive for a ninety-minute show."

"I assure you, it's quite worth it. The girls are sensational."

"This is good, Hendrik." Charles felt proud of his friend. "Page one-hundred-seventeen."

"Miss Gates. She is our specialist. I must warn you, she can be quite rough. She insists on meeting with her clients and interviewing them before taking any assignment and you must pay for the interview. One hundred dollars. If she accepts you as a client then you trust her to create a wonderful experience. Each episode is different and she doesn't tell you what's going to happen. Her fee is one thousand dollars, but an encounter with Miss Gates can last anywhere from an afternoon to a weekend."

"Fabulous." Charles felt breathless with excitement. "Have you tried any of them?"

"Of course. I work hard." Hendrik cleared his throat. "They had to audition to be included. A lot of girls didn't make it. I upset some pretty little girls. I promised next edition."

Charles told Hendrik about Aurora's breakdown and how he'd sent her away with her daughter. He asked Hendrik for a recommendation.

"You got the whole weekend," Hendrik said. "Why not try a few? I'll send someone over tonight. A surprise."

"That's grand." Charles shuddered.

"Ja. Let me know what you think."

Weekend

Angel Ray had been disappointing. She'd arrived wearing a
white leather mini-skirt and a vest with white high-heeled
cowboy boots and announced, the moment she walked through
the door, that she wasn't wearing any panties. That news did
vaguely arouse Charles, but he was distracted by the crepey skin
on her neck and her sun-damaged hands. Angel had a thick covering of blond downy-hair growing on her face, a result of her
age combined with years of steroid abuse, and her deep tan highlighted this unfortunate feature. She looked old and old had
never been Charles' thing.

They'd set up the table in the living room and Angel gave
him a standard deep-tissue Swedish massage. Then, using a lot
of oil, she was able to manipulate him into a fairly intense orgasm
but he'd had to keep his eyes tightly shut, and flip desperately
through his mental images of women and moments from his past,
in order to remain erect. The experience had left Charles cold.

Saturday had been much more fun. Kim and Andrea were
lightweights, very petite, and as excited about their work as pup-
pies with a chew toy. As a bonus Hendrik included Ladair, who
was off season and at 5'8" weighed at least 185. Ladair wore a

black trench coat and seemed embarrassed when she recognized
Charles from the gym, but the enthusiasm of Kim and Andrea,
and their eagerness to get started, carried the group through the
first awkward moments. They all went up to Charles' bedroom.
Kim and Andrea pulled off their black spandex dresses on the
staircase and were nude by the time Charles got to his bed. Kim
and Andrea bubbled with enthusiasm as they arranged the pillows
so that Charles would be propped up comfortably and able to
see and enjoy the goings-on. They tied his limbs to the four
corners of the bed with soft black velvet rope. Ladair hovered
by the door, still concealed beneath her coat, while the girls
moved the two easy chairs and table out into the hall. When the
area was clear they took from their gym bag a bottle of Johnson's
baby oil, Charles' favorite, and coated each other's bodies. Both
girls were tanned and tight and the oil on their skin looked beautiful. They stood in front of Charles and warmed themselves up
with kissing and the fondling of each other's breasts, then moved
out on the floor and began their wrestling demonstration. The
girls writhed and squirmed together like worms in a bucket and
Charles had been so delighted that he didn't notice that Ladair
had removed her coat until she joined him on the bed and began
coating his body with the oil. She looked splendid in the pink
baby-doll nightie and proved to be a lovely companion.

Kim and Andrea wrestled for almost two hours. Ladair split
her time between Charles and the wrestlers, sometimes sitting
on the girls and pinning them to the floor until they cried "UN-
CLE." She never took off her nightie, and Charles had been
impressed with her splendid timing. The three girls made a
lovely group. When they had finished and untied Charles he gave
them each a two-hundred-dollar tip.

*   *   *

The ringing of the phone awoke Charles at 6:30 on Sunday morning.

"This is Doughdee Gates."

Charles sat up in his bed, excited by her deep manly voice. "Yes, Doughdee."

"I'm going to church," she said. "When I'm finished I'm coming to you. Be ready."

Charles started to ask what time but she hung up.

The first order of business in Charles' thorough sex grooming was the flushing and washing of the descending colon. He wasn't sure what activities Doughdee had planned but he wanted to be ready. Charles took out his mother's beige-rubber douche bag; it was getting old, the rubber dry and cracking near the top where it hung on the showerhead. He would probably have to replace it soon and the thought made him sad. Charles filled it with warm water and a few drops of Dr. Bronner's peppermint soap. He liked the soapy burn and sharp tingling in his lower bowel and sphincter and the minty-fresh smell of Dr. Bronner's. He hooked up the bag, tested the flow through the long, wand-like plastic tip with the symmetrical holes running up and down the shaft—a lovely rectal fountain. Then he clamped shut the hose and lay down in the bathtub. There were several positions Charles could assume. The one he chose today was side-lying with the left arm comfortably placed under the head. With his right hand he guided the wand up into his body the full five inches, then he released the clamp and was instantly filled with the painful heat of Dr. Bronner.

Immediately, Charles felt the morning urgency to empty his bowels. He clamped off the water flow, climbed out of the tub, squeezing hard with his butt cheeks, and released himself into the toilet. Bowel movements always gave Charles a glorious sense of health.

He got back into the tub and filled his body with the contents of the hanging bag. He lay there on his side holding the water in, resisting the cramping, ignoring the dribbling leak, and realized he'd never measured the douche bag's capacity. How much water was he holding now? How much could he handle? He remembered the first time he'd stolen his mother's bag when he was in high school and used it in his anus and how he didn't wash the tip afterwards. The thought made him smile. Charles could feel the water traveling the loopy course of his intestines. Even though the water was warm, it felt cool there, deep within his body. He waited a full ten minutes, allowing his insides a good soak, then once again emptied himself into the toilet.

Next came his shower. He let the water run for a few minutes, washing away the leaked fecal juice on the bottom of the tub, then stepped in and scrubbed himself with the horsehair brush and oatmeal cleanser. He soaped his scrotum and considered shaving but decided the sparse covering of red pubic hair gave him a more manly appearance. He got out of the shower, skin pink from the scrubbing and the heat, clipped the hair in his nostrils, his ears, his nails. He brushed his teeth, flossed, and stimulated his gums. He put on his green silk robe and slippers, then went downstairs to wait.

Doughdee arrived wearing a sunflower-yellow suit with wide jet-black velvet lapels. The narrow skirt rode just below the knee and her big feet were jammed into low, sensible black pumps. She carried a mid-sized gray-plastic Samsonite suitcase with built-in handle and wheels. Her shoulder-length African queen black hair was tightly braided into neat rows that hung loose and finished with delicate silver beads. She stood over six feet tall and was heavier than in her photographs, her body smooth but firm. She looked like a man in women's clothes, a linebacker in a dress. Charles adored that look.

"I need to change," she said in her masculine voice before Charles had a chance to welcome her. "Where's the toilet?"

Charles led her down the hall to the guest powder room.

"Take off that silly robe, go in the living room, and wait for me on the couch." Doughdee shut the door in his face. "Sit on your hands," she yelled.

Charles hurried into the living room, drew the curtains, folded his robe and put it over the maroon velvet chair, then settled himself in the middle of the couch and dutifully sat on his hands, palms up so that they cradled his butt cheeks. His thin penis lay resting but alert on his leg, and Charles experimented with crossing and uncrossing his legs, trying to find the most flattering position. He decided on knees together, feet flat on the floor.

"You're a scrawny little thing," Doughdee said from the doorway. "Pale." She wore a heavy black velvet robe, with wide Dolman sleeves, that trailed as she walked. She was magical, a high priestess. Doughdee set her suitcase on the coffee table in front of the couch. "I hate pinky-white skin."

Charles was confused by the insult. Humiliation was a familiar game, he could play it well, but how did she want him to respond? Should he whimper?

"Put this on." Doughdee held up a pair of shiny black nylon exercise tights. "Be careful with the hole. I don't want any runs."

Charles wasn't sure which hole she was referring to but he didn't dare anger her further with silly questions. He carefully put his feet into the legs of the tights. Then, as he pulled them on, he saw that there was a quarter-sized hole in the crotch, a penis hole.

"You'd better be a good boy," she said as she watched him thread his penis through the hole and pull the tights up to his navel. "Don't make Mama angry." She handed Charles a pair of black socks.

Charles pulled on the black wool socks, careful to not make eye contact. Doughdee was strict; mustn't annoy her. He took the long-sleeved black nylon shirt she handed him and pulled it on over his head. The neck was tight and the hood fit snugly around his face. There were gloves attached to the sleeves and Charles had a tricky time getting his fingers in the right holes. When he had everything adjusted he looked up at Doughdee.

She studied him for a moment, then said, "You're gonna learn to be quiet." She took from her bag a black rubber ball, the size of a lemon, that had red ribbons attached on each side. "Tie it real tight."

Charles opened his mouth wide and fit the ball between his teeth. It was made of soft, chewy rubber and felt good to bite on. He ran the ribbons above his ears and fumbled with a bow at the back of his head. If the ball hadn't been in his mouth he would have smiled. Doughdee was such a strong leader.

"Sit on your hands."

She took from her bag a pocketbook-sized cassette player, set it on the table, and pressed Play. Soft, water sounds combined with wind chimes and flutes began to play as Doughdee removed her robe. She wore a bolt of sheer black silk wrapped many times around her body and as the music swelled from dreamy new age to a more dynamic force of nature, with tom-toms pulsing in the background, she began to unwrap herself from the cocoon. She moved to the music, hips swaying, big feet gently stamping to the rhythm of the tom-toms in a warlike Indian dance. With each unraveling Charles could make out more and more of her naked and awe-inspiring physique. He obediently sat on his hands, his penis fully erect. Doughdee seemed to be enjoying herself too until she looked up at Charles.

She stared at his penis. "That could ruin my whole day." She stopped the music, secured the fabric under her arm so that it didn't unravel any farther, and took from her bag a bottle of baby oil and the largest dildo Charles had ever seen. It was dark brown, veined and the length of her forearm, elbow to wrist, and the width of an ankle. The sight of it frightened and thrilled Charles.

Doughdee squirted some oil into her hand, then grabbed Charles' penis and coated it. Her hands were rough, the calluses quite stimulating. When his penis was glistening with oil, Doughdee held up the dildo so that Charles could see that it was hollow and filled with a textured rubber sleeve. The opening was about the size of a quarter and covered with brown ridges and nubs. Doughdee guided Charles into the limb-sized sex toy and he had to bite down hard on his ball to keep from ejaculating right then and there. She told him to lean back on the couch and then she tied the heavy dildo to the drawstring of his tights so that it wouldn't fall over.

"Later you can use it like a pump," she said. "Don't touch it now. And don't you dare come in it."

She went back to her dance and Charles sat on the couch, his flesh covered from head to toe in black and brown. There were several kinds of music: classical, big band, swing, rap. Doughdee moved well to each selection. Sometimes she used the fabric as a prop; sometimes she danced nude. It was all very erotic, but what moved Charles the most was the sight of himself with an overlarge brown penis.

Finally, Doughdee allowed Charles to manipulate himself and he grabbed the plastic bone and rode it up and down his rigid phallus. Charles had never experienced such sensation; he wondered if this was what the blow-up doll craze had been all about. Doughdee kept yelling "Don't come inside my sleeve," and Charles was just barely able to pull himself out at the last moment and release himself into the wad of paper towels that Doughdee had waiting.

*   *   *

Doughdee left the soiled wad of paper towels on the coffee table, packed her things in the suitcase, and walked naked to the guest bathroom. She didn't speak or acknowledge Charles in any way. Charles put on his robe and slippers, then went to the entry hall to wait. When she emerged from the bathroom in her Sunday suit Charles held out three hundred dollar bills. She snatched them out of his hand.

"Next time maybe we could do one of your 'episodes'?" Charles said respectfully. "Spend the weekend?"

"No." Doughdee stuffed the money into the side pocket of her suitcase. "You don't qualify."

"I beg your pardon?"

"You can beg all you want, sucker. I'm not interested in your business."

For a moment Charles was insulted, furious in fact, but then realized that they were still playing. He smiled, winked at her, and said, "Whatever you say, Mistress."

"I'm not joking, fool." She opened the front door. "I came here 'cause I owed Hendrik a favor. I've paid up now." She walked out and shut the door behind her.

THREE

Seven Weeks and Counting

Aurora's second eight-week cycle had been easy and fun. After shedding twelve quick pounds of water, her body tightened up. She'd quit the insulin, stayed on the growth hormone, and started on the Parabolin, Masterone, and those magical little Dianabol pills that were shaped like little pink stop signs. Her muscles swelled like yeasty dough in the oven, separate, hard and full. Her skin was less blemished and the light blond hair on her face and shoulders was easily managed with a gentle depilatory cream Charles ordered from Switzerland. Her clitoris had swelled and was very sensitive but she didn't mind. Charles kept her legs and genitals hair-free with a new hot wax kit he'd bought at the beauty supply. Aurora liked how she looked and it was cooler now without all that pubic hair. Her skin had the dusty smoothness of velvet.

With Aurora's new, impressive body came new prestigious friends. She'd been invisible to a whole group of bodybuilders but now they welcomed her. Each morning she'd walk into the gym and greet Amelia Lockwood or Ladair Simms or Cookie Lazar; they'd call out to each other in their deep manly voices, like doves cooing in a secret language. Sometimes the girls would go into the posing room and show each other body parts. They all said that Aurora had one of the best backs in the sport. People were complimenting her daily on her developing physique until Hendrik told her she had to cover up. "Too much exposure," he'd said. "Let's keep them guessing."

Aurora had her treadmill set up in front of the mirrored wall in her bedroom. She was nude. The overhead lighting highlighted her cantaloupe-round deltoids. She watched her legs grab and release as she took each step. She'd dropped another percent of body fat this week and her weight was holding steady. Some days she wanted to kiss Hendrik; sometimes she thought about fucking him.

"Why can't you wear clothes?" Amy stood in the doorway looking down at the carpet.

"Come in, honey." Aurora smiled. Amy wore the new denim skirt and vest they'd picked out from the mail order catalog. She looked almost cute with her hair pulled into pigtails.

"Can't you at least put on underwear?" Amy stayed still.

Aurora stepped off the treadmill, grabbed a black cotton G-string from her drawer, put it on, and carefully got back on the running machine. Adolescent girls were so shy.

"A bra?" Amy met her eyes in the mirror.

"Enough." Aurora smiled to let Amy know she wasn't really mad. "Come in. You look so cute."

Amy walked into the room and stood behind the treadmill. "Mom?"

They'd been getting along so well. Amy was getting fatter every day but at least she seemed happy. "What is it, my angel?"

"Can I get some cowboy boots? The short kind with a little heel?"

Aurora couldn't believe it. Amy never wore anything but old sweatpants and dirty T-shirts. "What color?"

"Red and black," Amy said without hesitating.

"I used to have a pair like that, with real pointy toes." Aurora looked at herself in the mirror and redid her ponytail. Her face was lean and hard. She looked younger now that she was shaping up.

"They have them at the mall," Amy said.

"How do you know?" Aurora looked at her daughter. She hadn't taken Amy to the mall in months. Amy didn't like to go shopping.

Amy scratched at her hair, messing up one of her pigtails. She seemed to be having trouble answering the question. "This girl from school has them," she said finally, and smiled as if proud of herself.

"What girl?" Aurora slowed the treadmill and studied Amy. She was wearing pink lip gloss. And her fingernails were clean.

"Someone on the yard." Amy seemed confident now. "I don't know her name."

Aurora smiled. Finally, Amy was making some friends. It was all coming together, just like she knew it would. "Baby, we'll go as soon as I finish training this afternoon."

"That's okay." Amy came and stood next to the treadmill. "You could just give me the money. I'll go after school. The bus goes right by there."

"Is that safe?"

"Definitely. Lots of kids hang out."

Aurora remembered when she was thirteen. Hanging out with Jessica Parks, smoking cigarettes, making fake joints with crushed up leaves and oregano, then selling them to Mandy Lincoln. Aurora smiled. Mandy Lincoln had told them, the next day, that she'd gotten really stoned and Aurora had laughed when she called Mandy an idiot and showed her the fake pot. Kids.

"Take a hundred dollars out of my purse." Aurora watched Amy get the money. It was as if her daughter was blossoming right before her eyes. She was going to be just fine. Soon there'd probably be talk of boys. "Your lunch is on the counter."

Amy waved as she left the room.

"Eat all your fruit and stay away from candy," Aurora called after her. There was no answer.

The Mall

Skip waited in his car behind the school bus. The children loaded, single file, up the steps and through the door; some laughing and talking with friends, others alone and isolated. Sweet lambs in a flock. Except that kids are cruel. Those pretty girls with the nice clothes could talk to that skinny pimpled girl. They could say hello. Let her sit with them. But they never would. They didn't see her and she hated them. She'd cover the whole group with gasoline if she could. Toss a match and watch them change their tune.

The bus pulled away from the curb and Skip drove forward. Amy sat alone on the bench. She'd finally worn a dress. Skip felt proud. Amy was still a long way off from being a lady but the dress was a start. He followed their routine and pulled up to the bus stop. Amy pretended to be surprised, then hopped in the car. Skip waited for her to buckle her seat belt.

"Got it." Amy pulled a hundred-dollar bill from her backpack and waved it in Skip's face.

"She say anything?" Skip said.

"She used to have the same exact kinda boots." Amy was looking at him. "Isn't that weird?" He kept his eyes on the road.

"When?" Skip sped up to pass the bus. He pretended to focus on driving.

"I don't know. When I was little." Amy dug in her backpack. "She was happy to give me the money." Amy pulled out a king-sized Butterfinger and tore off the wrapper. "I could maybe get you some too."

"Did she say where she got them?" Skip gave those boots to Jeanine after her twelfth week of training. It had shocked her. She blushed and said she felt bad taking such an expensive gift but she'd worn them every day. They were short ankle boots with just enough heel to make her calves pop. She was beautiful in those boots.

"All the money comes from Charles. Mom's got a bunch of hundreds in her wallet." Amy took a bite of her candy; it crumbled and a big chunk fell in her lap. "I'll get you a couple."

"I don't want her money," Skip said. He took a breath and forced his voice to stay casual. "She didn't tell you where the boots came from?"

"Savannah, I guess." Amy opened her pack and started hunting again. "Why?" She looked up at him.

Skip shrugged in a no-big-deal way and turned into the mall's parking structure. Amy pulled out a big movie-sized bag of Skittles and was about to tear open the wrapper.

"Try a TurboCarb bar." Skip held out his newest find. "It's peanut butter." For the last three weeks he'd been trying to get her away from the hard-core candy, offering her healthy alternatives. "You love peanut butter."

"I don't eat cardboard." She pushed Skip's bar away and gobbled a handful of candy.

Skip pulled into a parking spot and turned off the engine. "That junk will kill you." He said it with real concern. Amy could do permanent damage to her metabolism. She was getting fatter by the day.

"I already have a mama, okay?" She winked at him and got out of the car.

Skip took the key from the ignition, hid it under the seat, and followed Amy into the mall.

Amy didn't have any calves and she was clumsy walking in the heels. She paraded up and down in front of the two-foot high shoe mirror watching her feet, happy as a clam, and Skip pretended to share her enthusiasm. But it was depressing.

"Do you have a big mirror?" Amy asked the fat, old-grandfather salesman. Guy was sixty-five, easy. He was organizing the colors of the sock display and didn't look up. "Excuse me," Amy said sweetly.

The salesman wore a black-and-white striped shirt that looked like a too-small bogus soccer team uniform. His sloped, withered shoulders were narrower than his fat sagging gut. He had girl-sized feet. Loser; he probably shit in a bag. Put a fucking rope around his neck and hang him from the third floor railing here at the mall. Let him swing till his face turned blue. Put the rude-fuck out of his misery. He folded socks and ignored Amy.

Skip stood up, got in the man's face, and grabbed his wrist. "She wants a bigger mirror," he said, real quiet and mean.

The salesman dropped the socks and quickly led them to the back of the store, where there was a dressing room with a mirror. He held the door open so that Amy could stand back and see.

"They're great." Amy studied herself hard. "Right, Skip?"

Skip glared at the salesman, who said, "They suit you very nicely."

Skip carried the bag with Amy's old dirty tennis shoes. Amy teetered along next to him. They walked through the mall looking in the store windows. After a few minutes Amy got used to the new boots and walked more smoothly. Skip talked her into a diet soda today instead of a Coke and she seemed to like it.

Jeanine used to love Coca-Cola too. She showed up that first day at the gym with a plastic liter bottle of Coke in her gym bag. Skip explained to her about sugar and calories and Jeanine switched to diet that day. He never had to say it twice.

Jeanine was good in every way. Her body responded to his training like plants to sunshine and rain. Her ears were perfect little flowers blooming on that long, fine neck. And when she'd sweat there'd be gentle misty-wetness on her chest like sweet morning dew. Skip would sometimes poke her there, hard, on the chest, pretending to point out the separation between the upper and lower pec. Sometimes he hurt her a little but he had to be rough or she might realize that he was just wetting his finger in her freshness. He had to be close. He watched and waited for her to give him a sign, something that said she wanted him. But except for that one beautiful night, the most important of his life, she never let on. She was as cold and distant as that plastic bag full of his mother's chunky ashes. Sometimes, Skip dreamed about wrapping his fingers around Jeanine's neck, feeling her resistance as he squeezed her hard. He'd watch her struggle for breath, her face turning red, but then her neck would stretch and change into a snake that lunged and coiled around Skip's body until it was he who couldn't breathe.

Amy put her empty cup into Skip's hand. She'd chewed the straw all the way down to the plastic lid so now it was flattened and curled with bite marks. They were standing in front of a woman's clothing store. The mannequins had black wigs and were bone-skinny with slouchy hips and shoulders and had earrings threaded through their plastic nostrils and brows.

"You don't like skinny girls," Amy said.

"Nothing uglier than a starving woman." Skip wanted say he hated fat women too but they were having such a nice afternoon.

"Think I should dye my hair blond like my mom's?" Amy took out a bag of Big League Chew, gum made to look like chewing tobacco. She pulled long strings of pink bubble gum from the pouch and stuffed them into her mouth.

"Dyed hair always looks fake." Skip walked over to the trash can and threw out Amy's cup. "You couldn't get that natural look of your mama's."

Amy turned to face him. "She totally dyes her hair."

Skip smiled at Amy's ignorance. He put his arm around her shoulder. "I've known her a long time." He gave Amy a squeeze. The poor girl was so jealous of her beautiful mother. "Your mama is the real thing."

Amy pulled away from Skip. "Her real hair is darker than mine." Her voice was shrill. "Her pubic hair is black. Only now she doesn't have any 'cause she shaves it." Amy made a harsh laughing noise. "Those boobs. She's completely fake."

Skip felt like he was wearing a heavy wool sweater on the hottest Savannah day. He wanted to shake Amy. "Don't you ever talk about your mama like that." Little unappreciative bitch. He started walking fast back toward the ramp to the parking garage. Amy clumped along behind him. He stopped and faced the child. "Your mother is beautiful."

Amy looked confused. "I didn't mean anything." Her eyes were brimming with tears. "I'm sorry."

"Say you love your mother," Skip said in a stern voice. He had a duty to teach this child. Amy looked off in the distance, her eyes unfocused. Skip raised his voice, "Say it."

A woman with a baby in a stroller slowed down and stared. She studied Skip like he was some kind of a pervert.

Amy walked over close to Skip. "I love my mother," she whispered. Tears streamed down her cheeks.

"Of course you do." Skip patted her head. "We both do." He wiped her face with the bottom of his T-shirt and the two of them walked past the woman with the stroller and back to his car.

Five Weeks and Counting

Underwear, even the smallest G-string, ruined the lines of the faux-leather halter jumpsuit. It was made of shell-pink nylon and fit Aurora like shrink-wrap, all tight and shiny-wet looking. The back was cut in a low wide V and the bottom of it rode just above her butt crack. The gloss of the fabric highlighted muscle separation and definition better than skin; Aurora's legs looked Superhero-hard when she flexed them, shredded and beautiful. Humans weren't supposed to look like this but she did.

Aurora pulled on the jumpsuit carefully, so as not to snag the fabric. She fastened the three snaps at the neck, hit a front abdominal shot, and gazed at herself in true admiration. You could see everything. Her abs were perfectly etched, each lump separate from the rest. Aurora felt excited. She looked at her crotch. The jumpsuit highlighted her pussy, too; without the pubic hair to mask detail, the lips and distended clit showed through as clearly as her hip flexor tie-ins. Nice as it was to look at, Aurora couldn't walk around the gym like that. She went into the bathroom and got a roll of clear, two inch, heavy duty packing tape from the drawer. She took down her jumpsuit and pulled off a three inch long piece. Charles had just waxed her two days before and so there weren't any wispy hairs; her skin was smooth and very soft. Aurora stuck the tape just above her cleft and pulled it down over her meaty genitals. She molded the crackly adhesive over her clitoral ridge, past her vagina, and fixed it to the innermost crease of her ass. There was a nice supportive feeling with the tape. Aurora pulled the jumpsuit back up and studied her crotch. Perfect. Just like Barbie. She threw the tape into her bag, in case she needed to pee, and left for the gym.

Aurora waved at Leo and pulled into her parking place. Each morning, for the past two weeks, Leo had wheeled his trash can into the first spot next to the door and left it there while he pretended to clean in the area. When Aurora arrived he moved his can with a flourish and waved her into the privileged spot.

"Good morning, Mrs. Aurora." Leo bobbed his head when he talked and left his tongue lying on his bottom lip so he slurred whenever he spoke in his slow-dumb voice. He had black stringy hair, bulging eyes and the clammy, over-round fatness that made him look ageless, like a manatee. The gym let him clean the parking lot and the bathrooms inside.

Aurora waved and got out of her car. She bent over to get the gym bag from the backseat.

Leo panted. "Oh boy, oh boy, oh boy." He shifted from one foot to the next. "That's the prettiest outfit I ever seen, Mrs. Aurora." Leo's head and chest were bobbing together now.

Aurora straightened up. "Thanks for saving my spot." She punched Leo on the shoulder. Last week she'd made the mistake of kissing Leo on the cheek and he'd grabbed her and held on to her waist, burying his face in her chest. He was surprisingly strong and she had to use her knee and nudge him hard in the groin to get free. Once she was inside the gym she looked out and saw him dry-humping the air, his pelvis thrusting wildly and pumped with the overfiring of sexual impulse from his poor damaged brain. Leo's hands flapped at his sides like the spastic wings of a dying swallow, his mouth opened and drooling, head thrown back and bobbing in retarded ecstasy.

Today, Leo didn't touch her. He stood rubbing his shoulder where she'd hit him, grinning stupidly. Aurora walked away.

Aurora felt proud of her music. It had a strong primal beat and a woman panting fast and slow. The breathing sounded like singing and the drums made Aurora want to pose. Those sixty seconds of music meant strength and love and power, the sound of her body. It was beautiful. Hendrik thought the music obscene. He said it reminded him of the sound track to a porno movie. He told Aurora she should do her masturbating in private, that he was finished and going back to Germany if she used it in the contest. They'd had a big fight. Hendrik had disappeared and Aurora trained alone for three days. Luckily, Charles understood. He wasn't a Neanderthal; he was educated about art and music. Somehow, he finally got Hendrik to calm down and accept her choice. Aurora reached into her bag and felt for the cassette. It excited her to think about the routine.

Use of the posing room at the gym was by appointment only. When they first built it, it was opened to anyone, but people kept locking themselves in for long periods. There were suspicious dark stains on the floor mats and walls. The gym worried about sanitation and liability. Now you had to sign the key out and leave your license as collateral. The desk had the passkey and could enter at any time.

Aurora got a key and walked through the gym to the posing room. She had a nine o'clock appointment to do her routine for Cookie Lazar. Cookie won her pro card two years ago. She had blond hair like Aurora's only longer with the extensions. She was frequently in the magazines and had done a cover. Cookie was one of the few pros who trained alone. Aurora thought they looked alike and dreamed that one day they could be training partners. She fantasized about the magazine articles featuring the two beautiful blonds shining at the top of the sport. Cookie and Aurora, in matching bra-tops and short-shorts, demonstrating the proper form on side laterals or tricep extensions. The two women seriously encouraging each other, beautiful and intense. Those photographs would inspire men and women alike.

It could happen. Aurora and Cookie were becoming friends. It was an honor that Cookie had asked to see Aurora's routine. Aurora felt for her cassette again and hurried back to the posing room.

Cookie leaned against the wall next to the posing room door, waiting. She wore black fishnet stockings with a zebra G-string and matching zebra bra-top. Her stomach was tanned and her body was chiseled and tight.

"I love your outfit," Aurora said. She unlocked the door and let Cookie enter first.

"Trashy Lingerie." Cookie walked into the ten-by-ten foot room. "They've got way better stuff than Max Muscle or Body Alive." Cookie put her bag on the bench against the side wall, sat down, crossed her legs at the knees and studied Aurora. "That's nice. Is it rubber?"

"Nylon." Aurora closed the door and flipped on the bright overhead lights. She moved to the center of the room and tightened her legs. The detail of her musculature was even more pronounced under the intense, stagelike lighting.

"Let me feel it," Cookie said from the bench.

Aurora walked over and stood in front of the bench. Cookie stayed seated, reached up and ran her right index finger slowly down the center split of Aurora's abs, from solar plexus to just below the navel. It tickled and disturbed Aurora. She stared straight ahead at the wall behind Cookie.

"I love it," Cookie said. She reached out to Aurora's hip and molded her hand over the top of the right glute. "It looks great on you."

Cookie's eyes were smoky and soft. Were they sexy? Aurora moved away. She was aware of her secured genitals and there was a light throbbing beneath that tape. She hurried over to her gym bag and got out the cassette of her music. She was self-conscious with Cookie watching her. Clumsy. The tape machine was built into the opposite wall and she fumbled to load her music and turn it on.

"Did you bring a posing suit?" Cookie asked.

Aurora felt herself blush. She fiddled with the volume and shook her head.

"Why not? I wanted to see you."

"Next time I will." Aurora's voice was high and thin. Still facing away from Cookie, she twisted her hair up into a bun and secured it with a rubber band to show her whole back. Aurora pushed Play and assumed her position in the middle of the room. Her body looked good in the front wall-sized mirror, her symmetry perfect. She looked up at the hanging angled-mirror behind her and was pleased with the width of her back. She stood still, in a front relaxed pose, and waited. There was a long lead-in to the music and in those few seconds, with Cookie staring, Aurora felt her nipples stiffen. She worried that the wetness between her legs would loosen the tape. Then the music started and she forgot about everything.

At first it was a gentle pulse accompanied by a woman's soft panting. Aurora stared at herself and watched as she brought her straight-stiff arms slowly over her head, like a magnificent swan opening its wings. Her rigid fingers shot lightning-energy out into the air. A living sculpture. She held the position at the top, arms raised, body tight, until the music shifted and the heavy sex-drums led her into the next pose. Boom. She pulled her arms down and shifted her hip into a front double bicep. Somewhere, Aurora heard Cookie sigh in admiration but it didn't distract her. She swiveled her hips in a grinding move, three times, snapping into position with the rhythm of the music. The panting turned into heavy breathing. Aurora's hands popped open and she dropped them to her sides, then pulled them up her body, slow and sexy, and shifted into a side chest.

Cookie said, "Nice."

Aurora smiled at herself in the mirror. It *was* nice. She dropped to the ground in front splits, a move that would send most bodybuilders to the hospital, then twisted around into a back-lunging lat spread. Cookie moaned. Aurora came up out of the lunge and was just about to hit a back double bicep when the door burst open and Hendrik walked in.

"What is this?" he said.

Aurora turned off the music. "Cookie just wanted—"

Hendrik glared at Cookie. "Get out of here."

Cookie looked embarrassed. She stood, picked up her gym bag, and started for the door. Hendrik blocked her exit.

Cookie looked at the ground, defiant. Hendrik put his hand on her right shoulder and shook her firmly. "Keep away."

Cookie pushed past him without looking up or answering.

Aurora had recovered. There was nothing wrong with showing her posing routine to a friend. Fucking Hendrik. Aurora yanked her cassette and threw it into her bag. She whirled around, furious. "I can't have friends?"

Hendrik was angry too. "She's not your friend. I am your only friend till this is over." He wagged his finger at her. "You wear sweatpants and sweatshirt every day. NO ONE sees your body."

Aurora felt her strength crumble. She picked up her bag and started to cry. "I didn't do anything wrong." She wanted to lie down on those filthy floor mats and go to sleep.

Hendrik softened his voice. "You don't know what you were doing. These girls don't want you to win. You can't take any chances."

Aurora cried harder.

Hendrik came over and put his arm around her. "Five more weeks, little one. I'll put you on top of the world."

Aurora leaned into him and let herself sob. Hendrik patted her head with his other hand and let her cry.

Hungry

Amy opened the refrigerator. Each shelf was filled with different sized plastic containers, all labeled on matchbook-sized white stickers with date and time. The containers on the top shelf had blue lids and were marked for today. The next shelf down had green lids and were for tomorrow. Below that were the clear lids. On the bottom shelf there were a few old apples, a bag of salad, and some nonfat cottage cheese. Nothing to eat. Amy slammed the door. Aurora didn't even pretend to care anymore. She walked back upstairs to her room, pulled the brown paper bag from under her bed, and took out the box of frosted chocolate chip Pop-Tarts. She took the last foil pouch from the box, put it into her backpack and shoved the bag back under the bed.

"I'm leaving," Amy yelled from the hallway as she passed Aurora's door. She could hear the hum of the treadmill inside.

"It's early," Aurora called. She did not come out of her room. "Did you have breakfast?"

Amy was halfway down the stair. " 'Bye, Mom."

"Honey?" Aurora yelled as Amy slammed the front door.

*   *   *

Skip wasn't in his car. The windows were closed but the doors didn't lock so Amy got in the front seat to wait for him. The car felt warm and close with the dank but comforting smell of Skip. His green wool blanket sat neatly folded on top of his pillow in the backseat. Each night he slept within walking distance of Amy's house. He moved streets every couple of days, so that the neighbors didn't complain, but Amy always knew where to find him.

She took the foil pouch from her backpack and tore it open. Amy loved the crumbly crust and the sweet chocolatey filling. Pop-Tarts made her think of the pies that her grandmother made on Sunday afternoons. Grandma made extra dough so that Amy could make her own mini-pies in the special pie tins. The house smelled so good when they baked and sometimes they'd just have pie and cold milk for dinner. Skip and Pop-Tarts were the closest things Amy could get to home.

Skip came out from behind the bushes next to the car. Amy pretended not to see him; he was zipping up his fly. She focused on the second Pop-Tart and stuffed it into her mouth.

"What's for breakfast?" Skip got into the car and shut the door.

"She doesn't even pretend to care. The refrigerator is filled with her stuff." Amy swallowed her bite. She felt angry again. "She doesn't even have time to buy me food."

Skip started the car. "Next few weeks are going to be tough." He reached over and patted Amy's shoulder. "I'll get you through them. I promise."

Amy crumbled up the empty foil pouch and shoved it into her backpack. "Let's ditch school today. We could drive up the coast to this beach I know."

Skip shook his head and drove toward the school.

Amy fought back tears. "Please don't make me go." Tears leaked from her eyes. "Let me stay with you." Her nose started to run.

"Sweetie, we talked about this." Skip tore a paper towel from the roll under his seat. "But I promise you one thing." He waited while she blew her nose. "Things are going to get better real soon."

Making It Right

S kip hid in the bushes across from the semicircular high-rise apartment building. If something happened to Hendrik, Aurora would need a new trainer. There were less than five weeks till the contest, the most critical time in her preparation. She couldn't do it alone. Soon, with her dieting and her increased cardiovascular activity, she would turn into a zombie and her trainer would be absolutely essential. Aurora would look to him for support on all levels. She'd need him to reassure her on the days when she looked flat from lack of carbohydrates. She'd need him to carry her through her workouts when she felt discouraged and exhausted. He'd have to massage her aching muscles. He would have to drive her around when she got disoriented and light-headed. Her trainer would be her best friend for these last few weeks, and then, if she won, he'd be her hero.

Each morning, at 8:30, the uniformed doorman brought Hendrik's black Cadillac up from the garage. It was a high-security building; all exit doors had mounted video cameras and were bolted from the inside. The only way in was past the doorman and the guard at the elevators. Skip wasted twenty bucks on flowers to learn that all deliveries had to be left with the doorman.

The guy at the gym had laughed and said, "Tell me something I don't already know," when he called and told him that Hendrik was a drug dealer. The police wanted Skip to identify himself. They weren't interested in anonymous reports.

Hendrik's stupid car alarm went off whenever Skip tried to mess with the brakes. He'd almost been caught there in front of Charles' house when Hendrik came running out to see what was going on.

He couldn't poison Hendrik's food 'cause what if Aurora took a bite? He wasn't sure he could take Hendrik down with a knife.

Skip hadn't touched his gun since the drive cross-country. He'd been bored and picked up a hitchhiker. Turned out the fucker was a fag and when he reached over to touch Skip's leg, Skip pulled his gun and stuck it in the asshole's crotch. He pulled the car over, let the fairy get out, then started shooting, close enough to make fudge-packer shit his pants. God damn hilarious. Guns were always effective.

Hendrik hugged the doorman, same as every morning, and got into his car. He opened the mirror on the visor and adjusted his hair, like a god damn woman, then started the engine. Skip closed his left eye and aimed. There was a lot of traffic on Lincoln, and Hendrik had to wait. Skip held his arms out, both hands on the gun, steady and straight; excitement made him calm. As Hendrik pulled into traffic, Skip focused on his right ear and squeezed off a shot. *Click.* Nothing happened. He fired again, this time at the whole head with both eyes open, but the fucking gun was broken and Hendrik drove away.

A Long Night for Amy

Amy kissed her mother good night, turned off the light on her bedside table, pulled up the covers and waited. She heard Aurora shut off the light in the hallway and close her bedroom door. After half an hour, at 11:00, she crawled out of bed and changed into the denim skirt and vest that were hidden under her bed. She grabbed her backpack with her schoolbooks and took out the note. It said:

> *Mom,*
> *Got up early to go to the library. I've got a report due. See you tonight,*
> *Amy*

Carrying her boots, she crept down the hall and stopped at her mother's door. It was dark and quiet. She slid the note under the door, snuck along the wall, avoiding the creaky boards in the middle of the floor, and down the stairs. She punched in the code on the alarm, opened the door, and left. The fog felt icy-wet on her bare legs and arms. She ran across the lawn and by the time she got to the sidewalk her socks were soaked with water and mud.

Skip was parked in a shadowy area, away from streetlights, under a tall spreading eucalyptus. There weren't many cars on this tree-lined street. Most of the houses were gated and set back from the road, obscured behind hedges.

When Amy rounded the corner and saw the rusting gold Honda sitting on the darkened street she felt the icy-sickness in her stomach melt away. She ran fast down the street, excited and eager to surprise Skip. He would be thrilled to see her, rush to take her in his arms, twirl her around and kiss her on the cheek. He'd think she looked beautiful. More beautiful than Aurora. They'd hold hands and talk and laugh. Skip was lonely too. He'd see that she wasn't just a little kid. She was almost a woman and she could take away his loneliness.

As Amy got closer she slowed and hunched down. She had to suppress a giggle; she felt giddy. He was going to be so happy. She knelt by the rear bumper trying to decide between jumping up and yelling "Surprise" or pounding on the roof and yelling "Boo." As she crouched there, quiet, she heard Skip's voice.

"Lucky motherfucker."

Amy knew it was Skip in that car talking but she didn't recognize the angry-loud voice. It scared her.

"Cut off your arms and shove 'em up your flat German ass." He laughed, ugly and sarcastic. "You're dead." He paused. "I'M GONNA FUCKING KILL YOU."

Amy crawled back on the sidewalk and pressed herself against the ficus hedge, hidden in the shadows. She listened hard. The car and the street were still. She wanted to undo what she'd heard. She didn't want to know about the dark part of Skip; she willed it to go away. Amy stood in the quiet of the night and was sorry she'd come. She stood for what seemed like hours, unsure of what to do. She was cold with bare arms and legs and wet feet. Maybe he was dreaming.

Finally she called out, "Skip?"

He didn't answer. She moved up next to the car window. Amy could make out his sleeping form in the front seat. She gently knocked on the roof. "Skip?"

Skip bolted up; his right hand fumbled for something under the seat. He stopped when he saw her. "Amy?"

Amy nodded, afraid she might cry. She needed him to be happy; she felt she would die if he didn't smile. She waited, bracing herself for his response.

"What are you doing out here, my little angel?" He got out of the car and gave Amy a hug. It felt warm and safe. She was so relieved she leaned into him and closed her eyes.

"Did something happen?" he said.

Amy shook her head.

Skip put his hands on her shoulders and looked into her face. "Did you rob a bank or something?"

Amy giggled.

Skip held her there, looked at her, and waited for an answer.

She felt shy and said in a soft voice, "I thought we could have a sleep-over?"

Skip studied her in the dim light, like he was trying to figure out where she came from and what kind of creature she actually was. He hugged her again, then led her to the sidewalk. They sat there for a while, quiet. Skip had his arm around Amy's shoulders and it made her feel calm. Sleepy.

Finally he said, "Baby kitty, there is nothing I like more than your company. And I am honored that you'd consider having a sleep-over with boring old Skip." He stroked her hair. "But, little darling, we could both get in a whole lot of trouble if they find you out here."

Amy said, "No one cares where I am."

"Your mama'd be real worried if she knew you were gone."

"Bullshit." It was the first time Amy had ever sworn in front of Skip and it made her feel grown-up and strong.

"She loves you, baby." Skip sounded like the fat-assed principal at her school, full of shit and out of touch.

Amy pulled away and tried to stand up but Skip held her tight. She hated him.

"Few more weeks and your mama's gonna be right back to her old self." He kissed her hair. "She needs you now."

"She doesn't." Amy started to cry. "Can't I stay with you?"

Skip wiped her tears with his hand. "You are the most precious thing in the world to me. You and your mama. When you have trouble sleeping, or you're missing me, remember that old Skip is just outside. And I'll always be here for you." He kissed her on the forehead.

Amy unlocked the front door, turned the alarm back on, and snuck up the stairs. She opened her mother's door a crack, grabbed the note, went to her room and ripped the note into tiny confetti-pieces.

Charles Loved Doughdee

The day after his encounter with Doughdee, Charles went to the Garden Jungle florist and picked out two hundred dollars of exotic flowers. The tropics produce the most frankly sexual flora and fauna. Charles hoped Doughdee would appreciate the overlarge blood-red stamens and the vulvalike fuschia petals of his colorful bouquet. He wrote "Thank You" and signed his name on the simple card. Charles had the gift delivered and spent the rest of that day waiting for some acknowledgment. None came. He called the florist the next day to verify delivery and found the flowers had been received and signed for by Doughdee Gates.

The next weeks were a flurry of gifts. Food baskets, lingerie, champagne, jewelry, all were received and signed for and none were acknowledged. Charles sent daily letters. At first they were dignified, even witty, but when Doughdee didn't answer Charles had no choice but to grovel. Still no word.

Then one morning Charles woke up happy. He realized that this pain, this terrible humiliation was all part of Doughdee's marvelous plan. He knew that one day soon she would arrive at his door and free him from the agony and that together they

would ascend to new levels of enlightenment. Brilliant Doughdee, she understood him like no other. He was willing to endure
whatever torture she prescribed. She was a genius. Charles threw
himself into the role of the willing student and called Doughdee's
house daily. She never answered the phone but he left long messages on her machine begging her to rescue him. Sometimes he'd
break down and sob. The machine would cut him off after thirty
seconds and so he'd have to call back as many as five times to
finish his thoughts.

There were moments of fear. What if he was wrong? Sup-
pose Doughdee was laughing at him? What if she didn't care?
Those times of doubt jolted his body with electric pain and left
him exhausted. He'd nap then and usually when he awoke,
he felt better. No one could be that cruel, certainly not his
Doughdee.

Aurora continued to come to the house each morning for
her drugs, posing, skin care and depilation. Her body progressed
according to schedule. Hendrik felt confident she would win.
Charles feigned excitement at her development, but next to
Doughdee's exotic spice, her brilliant flavors, Aurora was waxy-
orange American cheese and held little interest for him. Charles
halted their sexual relationship. He preferred to be alone with
his Doughdee-thoughts during those frequent moments of
arousal. He told Aurora that all her energies must now go to
contest preparations.

On the day he left the message that he was going to kill
himself if Doughdee didn't come to him soon, Charles hung up
and was stunned. It was true; he couldn't go on much longer. He
sat on his bed, looking at the phone, listening to the quiet of his
house, and realized that his life was nothing unless this woman,
this hard, intelligent beauty would join him. She was what he'd
been searching for his entire life. Her strength and her wisdom.
If he couldn't have her, Charles Worthington wouldn't go on.

He lay back on the bed, calm, and considered his options. He would never do anything as messy or inconsiderate as shooting himself or slitting his wrists; those were selfish options, quite unfair to Mrs. Johns. Breathing exhaust fumes seemed dirty. Self-asphyxiation must, at some point, be uncomfortable. No. Charles would medicate. A lovely bottle of wine, cognac and a handful of potent tranquilizers, absolute serenity. He smiled as he drifted into his nap, happy with his new plan.

Charles was awakened by the insistent ringing of his doorbell. It was getting dark outside and he was disoriented. He'd slept all afternoon. Charles pulled his green silk robe tightly around his body and hurried down the stairs. At the door he asked who it was over the intercom.

Hendrik sounded worried, even panicked. "Are you all right?"

Charles was confused, although touched, by his friend's concern. Of course, he was all right. He opened the door and there, standing next to Hendrik, was Doughdee. Tall and excellent in a black velour cat-suit and purple leather pumps. She stood at Charles' door and she was looking at him with what? Concern? Fear? Was it, possibly, love? Charles was overcome with the most intense joy; for a moment he was speechless. He wanted to drop to the ground and kiss those big black feet, lick at the meaty toes that were so artfully jammed into the cruelly pointed heels.

"You're here." His voice was filled with wonder, tears welled in his eyes. He looked deeply into Doughdee's eyes so that she'd know he understood. "I knew you'd come to me."

Doughdee turned to Hendrik. "See?"

Hendrik ignored Doughdee and said in an angry voice, "Why didn't you answer phone?"

What was Hendrik talking about? Why was he here interfering with the most important moment of Charles' life?

"I call you for hours." Hendrik put his hand on Charles' shoulder and gave it a shake. "That stupid machine answers." With each word he shook harder, accenting his anger. "Over and over, I call."

"I was napping." Charles moved back into the house, out of Hendrik's reach. He looked to Doughdee and asked her, "What is this?"

Doughdee ignored Charles and said to Hendrik, "Can I go now?"

Hendrik stepped into Charles' entry hall and said, without turning around, "Get out of here." He slammed the door with his foot and led Charles by the elbow into the living room.

"Where's she going?" Charles felt he was spinning in a horrible nightmare. He was sick with confusion. Abandoned. His mother used to leave him, alone and needy, while she went to her luncheons and cocktail parties. He'd stay in his room, curled on his bed, waiting for hours to hear the sound of her Jaguar pulling into the garage. She'd never come up to him. He'd rush from his room, down the stairs, and welcome her back, hugging her. She'd pry his little arms off and often scold him for wrinkling her dress. "You're too old for such foolishness."

Hendrik lowered Charles onto the couch and sat down next to him. "She calls and plays this crazy message." Hendrik shook his head. "She is laughing." He put his arm around Charles' shoulder. "You scare me."

Charles could hear Hendrik's voice but it seemed far away. He heard the word *laughing* but he couldn't attach any meaning to it.

"She tells me about the gifts, the letters." Hendrik held Charles tightly. "What are you thinking about with this filthy whore?"

Charles looked in his friend's eyes and felt the very foundation of his being collapse. He buried his face in Hendrik's shoulder, and cried. With each racking sob he mined the depths of his anguished childhood, his loneliness and fear. Each wail released new deeper pain. The tortured isolation of his shallow, meager life. It was too much. He pounded Hendrik's chest with his fists and allowed himself to be rocked back and forth.

"Shhhhhhh." Hendrik patted his back. Then, after a few minutes Hendrik said, "Enough. Put yourself together."

Charles stumbled to the powder room and splashed cold water on his red, blotchy face. He sat on the toilet and blew his nose. All his letters, the carefully selected gifts. He'd shared with her the secrets of his life. His dreams for the two of them. It could have been so beautiful. But Doughdee laughed at him. She used him and made him a fool. She was a whore. How had he been so blind? The embarrassment stung and changed his love for her to hatred in an instant. He walked out of the bathroom angry and strong.

"You'll fire her, of course." Charles stood in the doorway of the living room. Hendrik was still sitting on the couch. "Force her to leave town."

"You're better now?" Hendrik came and stood next to Charles. "Good." He hugged Charles. "We all make mistakes."

"Have you had her checked for diseases?" Charles pulled out of the embrace. "She could ruin your entire business." He sighed with relief. "Thank God I didn't take it any further."

"You need to eat a good dinner and sleep." Hendrik started toward the kitchen. "You like, I fix you something?"

Charles followed him. "You *will* fire her."

"Don't worry about it." Hendrik opened the refrigerator. "Maybe some nice eggs. Milk."

"Give me your word."

"She's my busiest girl." Hendrik faced Charles and looked apologetic. "Brings in a lot of money."

"I'll give you triple what she's worth." Charles paused and watched Hendrik do the calculations. "I'll write the check now."

Hendrik nodded happily and said, "She's gone."

Back in the Saddle

Charles was the conductor of a symphony orchestra, the general of a highly trained army, the high-stepping, baton-twirling leader of a lavish parade. The last few weeks of contest preparation would bring out the genius in him. He had built his champion, avoided most of the dangerous pitfalls, and Aurora was going to win. It was just a matter of fine-tuning. Charles regretted the foolishness over Doughdee. It had kept him away from Aurora. But he was back now and about to present the world with an absolutely superior female form. Aurora the magnificent.

At Charles' insistence, Hendrik picked up Aurora each morning and brought her to the house. Charles didn't want her driving. When she arrived the men studied her body and discussed the effects of her now extremely restricted diet. Each of the final five weeks served as a trial contest preparation. Sunday through Friday her diet would be adjusted and the results studied on Saturdays. The first week they'd been far too generous with the carbohydrates and Aurora looked full but smooth on that first Saturday morning. Aurora had cried and cried, saddened by the apparent loss of her hard-won definition. It took an hour for the men to convince her that it was merely the spillage of carbohydrate that created the water-logged appearance. A problem easily fixed.

The next week they'd cut her carbs in half, taking her to zero on Tuesday and Wednesday, and limiting her to three small cups of white rice on Thursday. She'd been shaky and forgetful all week but was shredded on Saturday morning and thrilled with her new physique.

"She's perfect." Charles couldn't help but state the obvious. It was so nice to see Aurora smile again. She stood on the platform and ran through her compulsory poses, sinewy steel-cabled muscles pumped full with blood. She was everything Charles had dreamt of. The decreased carbohydrates had drained her body of excess fluids, and while her muscles weren't quite as round, she was deeply shredded. No one would be more ripped on contest day and with her exquisite symmetry she was sure to win. He clapped his hands. "We've done it."

Hendrik let out a loud sigh and shook his head. Aurora stopped posing. Charles looked to his friend, confused.

"Too depleted." Hendrik studied Aurora for another minute. "Judges aren't going for extreme look this year."

Charles couldn't believe his ears. "Are you crazy?" He walked up onto the platform and pointed to Aurora's quadriceps. "The cuts between her muscle are an inch deep. She looks fantastic."

"That was good last year. Now they want more natural look." Hendrik picked up his bag and took out the camera. "We'll get it right." He pointed to Aurora and she assumed a relaxed frontal pose. He took her picture, then motioned for her to turn around so he could photograph her back. "Increase carbohydrate and fats, fill her out a tiny bit more."

Charles was angry; Aurora looked exactly the way he'd

wanted her to. "The leaner the better," he said. "Audiences love that anatomy chart look."

"Not this year." Hendrik lowered the camera and looked at Charles. "They want a fuller, more feminine look."

Charles was adamant. "I disagree." He came down off the platform and stood next to Hendrik. "This sport is about extremes. We should take her as far as we can."

Hendrik shook his head again, impatiently. "It's a drug look. They're moving away from that. You gotta believe me."

Charles was frustrated and torn. He knew he had to trust Hendrik but it hurt. "I love how she looks."

Hendrik put the camera back in his bag and said to Charles, "You'll love her next week too." Hendrik turned his attention to Aurora. "We'll get it right. Three more weeks. Plenty of time."

Three Weeks and Counting

The cold congealed fillet of sole that was Aurora's breakfast, with its fishy essence that stayed on her fingers and was excreted in her sweat, made her sick. It was as offensive as the thought of eating her waste or sampling her own clotted menstrual blood. She couldn't face it. She couldn't chew another bite of the foul sea protein. She took the premeasured fish, dumped it into the blender with water, ice cubes, and four packs of Equal, and liquefied it. She poured it into a twenty-ounce clear plastic cup, drank the cold putrid concoction in four big gulps, then rinsed her mouth with water from the kitchen faucet.

Breakfast was the toughest meal of the day. It was when she most longed for a muffin or a lovely piece of buttered sourdough toast. Three more weeks. Aurora had been keeping a list for two months of all the foods she craved and dreamt about. When this contest was over she intended to systematically eat everything on that list starting with the cheese enchiladas and working straight through potato chips with French onion dip, Skittles, German chocolate cake, nachos with extra sour cream, every kind of Winchell's doughnuts, Butterfingers, cheeseburgers, fries, pizza, boxes of Sees candy, taquitos, and M&Ms. She'd finish up with a half gallon of chocolate chip ice cream. Aurora would eat until she was sick with sugar and fat and there was nothing left that her body wanted.

Charles came and supervised the workouts now. It was nice. Aurora liked how he carried her bag and kept curious gym rats from getting too close. A lot of normal people, who hung around the gym and put together lumpy little-muscle arms with a skinny vein running down the bicep, considered themselves real body-builders. They wanted to talk contest preparation even though they'd never enter a show. They came up to Aurora and Hendrik in the middle of workouts to offer advice or talk strategy. Charles kept them away without being offensive. He didn't want Aurora to alienate her audience. She needed her fans.

What Aurora Saw

Aurora took a hold of Amy's arm and yanked it hard. It felt like the leg of a turkey held to the body by thick ligaments and skin, her wrist thin and bony like the end of a drumstick. Aurora would have torn that arm off if she could have. The arm held fast and Amy's body came tumbling out of Skip's shithole car and onto the sidewalk. Aurora wanted to kick her daughter. She grabbed the backpack of books from the front seat and threw it across the sidewalk, then leaned into the car and grabbed Skip's forearm in her fingernails, squeezing until she felt the flesh pop and her fingertips got wet with his blood. "You're going to jail, sick fuck."

Amy was crying and pulling on her other arm. "Mama, don't hurt him."

Aurora let go of Skip, turned, and shoved Amy away from the car. "Get in my God damn car."

Amy threw herself on Aurora. "Leave him alone." She tried to pull Aurora away. "He's my friend."

Aurora took hold of Amy by the shoulders and pushed her away, hard. Part of her knew that this wasn't the child's fault but rage had a hold of her. Amy fell on her ass and cried with sobs of a little girl. Whatever this sick relationship was about, Aurora felt betrayed. Amy had brought the past alive and was putting it right back in her face. Her daughter looked like the enemy sitting there on the ground.

Skip got out and ran over to help Amy stand up. They were being watched now by the kids waiting to board the bus. Aurora saw a security guard start to walk toward them. She grabbed Amy around the waist, picked her up, and carried her to the car. Amy was limp, sniveling.

The security guard, barely out of high school with blemished skin and arms thick as boulders, asked what was going on.

Aurora didn't stop. "That man molested my daughter."

Skip stared at Aurora but said nothing.

Amy tore free. "No." She kicked Aurora in the shin. "He's my friend. You're crazy."

Aurora stood still, ignoring the pain in her shin. There would be a bruise but it would probably be gone by the contest. "Amy, if you don't fucking get in the car right now I will call the police and have your boyfriend locked up for the rest of his life."

Amy hesitated. She looked to Skip.

"I'd never hurt that child." Skip took a step forward. "You know me, Jeanine."

Aurora shouted to Amy, "Get in the car. Now." She waited for her to close the door, then said to Skip, "If I ever see you again you're dead, you perverted piece of shit."

Aurora drove away.

What Amy Saw

Amy twisted around in the seat and watched Skip get in his car. Her mother was talking, yelling in fact, but Amy didn't hear. She was finished with listening. She felt her mother's evil hand clawing at her back, trying to turn her around. She ignored it, clutched the headrest, and kept her eyes fixed on Skip. He was behind them and she could see his face, angry and brave.

Aurora drove fast. The engine whined and the Porsche jerked as it swerved in and out of traffic. Skip kept up, his little car right on their bumper. He would save Amy. Someday they'd laugh about it together. Aurora would be dead or locked in some horrible stinking jail where she couldn't steal anything more from Amy's life. She'd rot and her teeth would fall out and she'd have to shit in a bucket. The thought made Amy strong.

They raced along the city streets, then turned down the hill that led to the Pacific Coast Highway. They stopped at the red light and Skip stopped behind them. Amy wanted to cheer when she saw Skip open his door and get out of his car.

Aurora screamed "Shit!" when she saw him heading toward them. She shifted the car into gear and, without looking to see if it was safe, turned left onto the highway against the red light.

Skip tried to follow. He ran back to his car and drove it right out on that highway. He didn't see the truck but Amy did. She saw the big red TEXACO sign on the side of the silver tanker. She saw the truck climb over and crush Skip's car like a flimsy aluminum soda can. She saw the truck flip over with Skip's car stuck to its wheels like a piece of gum on the bottom of a shoe. Amy saw the crash but heard no noise. She knew she was screaming, but Amy couldn't hear anything.

Skip Is Dead

"**M**other . . ." Aurora tried to be patient. "The little slut was sleeping with him."

Eileen inhaled sharply, then was quiet for several seconds. Finally, in the saddest voice Aurora had ever heard, Eileen said, "She's a baby."

"She won't talk. Lies in bed all day. I don't even know if she pees." Aurora took a drink of water, set the glass down on the kitchen counter, and willed herself not to cry. "Contest is less than three weeks away. I just can't handle it."

"I'll come and bring her back home."

"I'll pay for your tickets." At that moment Aurora loved her mother more than any other time of her life. Everything was going to be all right.

"Of course you will." The sharpness was back in Eileen's voice. "Now, put that sweet angel on the phone."

Dream Come True

When Grandma walked into her room, Amy thought she was dreaming. How could Grandma be here? Only ugly stuff happened in this ugly world. But when Grandma touched her forehead and said her name, Amy knew it was real. She sat up, happy. "Is she dead?"

Grandma looked confused. "Who?"

"Aurora." Amy grabbed her grandmother's hand and felt reassured by the truth of her dry warm skin. "Did she have an accident or something?"

Grandma spoke in a quiet and sad voice. "Of course not."

"Then why are you here?"

"I'm taking you home to live with me." Grandma helped Amy from her bed.

"She's letting me go?" Amy stood up. Her clothes felt warm and clammy. She'd been in bed for days.

Grandma nodded with tears in her eyes.

"Just like that?" Amy didn't trust it. Her mother had taken away everything in her life. She was afraid to be happy. "She knows you're here?"

"She called for me, honey." Grandma hugged Amy. She smelled powdery and soft.

Amy didn't ask any more questions. She got her stuff and walked out of that house in the boots she'd bought with Skip. Aurora wasn't home to say good-bye.

Three Days and Counting

Charles moved Aurora into his house. The last weeks of contest preparation were tricky. Many a bodybuilder had cracked in the final days, some throwing themselves into unstoppable eating binges. Fatty carbohydrates often looked like medicine to those plagued by the fear of failure. Charles didn't want to take any chances. Now, with that irritating child out of the way, there was no reason why Aurora shouldn't be under his constant supervision.

Charles and Hendrik had arrived at the perfect food combination. Aurora would be slightly softer, but fuller on contest day. Charles had to trust Hendrik's judgment. Now all they had to do was keep Aurora calm and on track. Charles put her on Catapres, a beta-blocker, so that she wouldn't hold any extra water due to nervousness. With this new drug, Aurora was a little docile, at times even dopey, but nicely relaxed.

Charles helped Aurora into the tanning bed and set the timer for forty-five minutes. She lay down, nude, and he carefully placed two wet cotton balls over her eyes before pressing the button to lower the top of the clamshell-like machine. Usually, Aurora would use a fan at the foot of the bed, a nice cooling device that allowed her more comfort. But Charles had removed the fan. This was a perfect opportunity for Aurora to sweat. To rid herself of excess water. The bulbs were new and the temperature rose well above one hundred degrees and Aurora would emerge from this session brown and vascular. An arousing sight indeed, one that would undoubtedly lead to playful coupling. Aurora, slick and sweating. Hard, warm, and bigger than life. Charles hurried to his bedroom. He wanted to prepare while Aurora baked. This was her final tanning session. Sun damaged the skin and caused it to retain water so it was prudent to stop tanning at least three days before a contest. From here on out they'd rely on Protan, a messy stainlike solution that had to be painted on the skin with a sponge-brush, left to dry for twenty minutes, then showered off and reapplied repeatedly like varnish until the desired color was achieved. Protan stained the tongue.

Charles had found that beans cooked with okra produced an abundance of gas in most people, but Aurora was close to her contest and beans were not on her program so he had to make do with raw cabbage. An hour before he loaded her into the tanning machine, he fed her half a head of red cabbage. He didn't allow Aurora to help, she had to sit helpless like a child, or perhaps an animal, while he spoon-fed her diced cabbage and sips of water. When her body was absolutely stuffed with roughage, he oiled her and put her in to bake.

Charles showered quickly. He soaped and scrubbed every part of his body so he'd be clean and fresh smelling. He brushed and flossed his teeth, trimmed his nose hair, put on his green silk robe, and hurried back downstairs to the tanning room.

The lights shut off and the top of the bed automatically lifted. There Aurora lay, in a clear pool of her own sweat. She glistened, brown and red. Charles removed the cotton balls from her eyes and helped her to stand. He could feel the intense heat from her body. He quickly led her to the daybed, where he helped her to lie, facedown, with her legs hanging off the end so that her glorious rump was fully accessible. Then Charles knelt behind her, spread the cheeks of the buttocks, pressed his nose against her sweet anus and waited to smell the divine essence that was Aurora.

Show Time

After weigh-in Aurora put her sweat suit back on. She sat in the corner of the drafty backstage dressing room with her feet up on a chair. Most of the other girls wore just their posing suits and were lined up in front of the makeup mirrors, adjusting their hair and makeup or reapplying Protan. So far, Aurora hadn't seen anything that worried her. There were some big heavyweights but none of them had her symmetry or hardness. There were a couple of girls she'd not seen yet but so far this was a piece of cake.

Eleanor Stubbs pulled off her sweatpants, sat down bottomless on a beige plastic folding chair, opened her legs wide and carefully removed the two gold earrings she had stuck through her inner labial folds. She stood and taped her cleanly shaved pubis securely with duct tape, then put on her lime-green posing suit. No one seemed the least bit surprised or interested in Eleanor's privates. Most of the girls at the national level needed some form of camouflage. There was nothing shameful in it. Aurora's yellow posing suit had a custom sleeve sewn inside the front panel that held the thin plastic liner-shield. The insert was slightly curved and cupped her mound beautifully, masking the elongated clitoris.

The backstage time used to be torturous for Aurora. She used to worry about stepping onstage, her music, the audience. She'd vomited at her first two shows, although that might have had something to do with the cheap wine she was drinking in an attempt to control her nerves and promote vascularity. Today she was calm. This contest was hers. The more she saw the better she felt. No one could stand next to Aurora.

Each girl had a different recipe for vascularity and fullness. Aurora stuck with peanut butter and a half teaspoon of all-fruit strawberry jelly. Erica Stern was eating white processed sugar. She held three packets together, tore off the tops, and poured the sugar directly into her mouth. When she threw her head back and shook the paper envelopes in an effort to get every last grain, the fat at the top of her thighs jiggled. How could anyone get onstage with that kind of shake? Aurora would rather die. Erica Stern had a huge chest and a shredded back, but loose legs were the kiss of death. She might as well go home.

Monica Lawrence was eating a Snickers bar. Monica had legs. Monica had arms, chest, and even a nice upper back. But nothing Monica did, no matter how hard she trained, would ever erase that thick trunklike torso. She could try to hide behind twisting poses but she'd never be in Aurora's league. It was a gift that she'd made it this far.

Jennifer Sloane was sucking on a family-sized bottle of Aunt Jemima Maple Syrup, while Karen List sprayed her back and shoulders with Pam. You'd think at the national level Karen would have learned about Pam. It was too shiny. The lights reflected off the oil like sunlight on the ocean. Judges practically had to wear sunglasses to look at a contestant wearing Pam. She was good but she wasn't in Aurora's league.

The room smelled of Preparation H. Everyone used it on their softer parts, lower abs, and thighs, to draw out subcutaneous water. It was a familiar smell, one Aurora associated with winning.

The lightweights were called for prejudging. Middleweights and heavyweights were pumping up with the dumbbells in the middle of the room. Some did push-ups, some ran through their posing routines. It was time to prepare.

Aurora stood and unzipped her sweatshirt. The air felt cool on her skin; that was fine. Those stage lights would hit her like a furnace; her muscles and veins would explode with the heat. She slid off the loose fitting sweatpants. Charles had cut out the elastic in the waist and ankles so that she wouldn't have to worry about lines from the clothing. Aurora grabbed the Bain Du Soleil gel, squeezed some into her palm, and starting with her feet, rubbed the orange oil into her skin. She hadn't shaved since Thursday. Shaving irritated the skin and could make it hold water, and she could feel the nubby sharpness of her hairs poking up through the skin. She could feel it but no one could see it.

She oiled the front of her body, careful not to put it on too thick or unevenly. She looked around to find someone to do her back and saw a dikey contest coordinator standing by the door dressed like a bus driver in blue synthetic pants and a light blue shirt. The woman was fat, her frosted hair cut short and spiky on top with a long rattail down the back. She tried to look official, answering questions and keeping fans out. Aurora could see she loved the job. She was an expert at applying oil.

The middleweights left for the stage. Aurora stepped over to the weights. She picked up some twenty-pound dumbbells and did a quick set of thirty curls. She could feel her pump immediately. She dropped the dumbbells, got down on the floor, and did a set of fifty push-ups. The other girls were talking and laughing but Aurora didn't participate. She walked over to the mirrors and even in the harsh flattening light of the makeup mirrors she was thrilled with her own magnificence. She looked around at the other heavyweights. Not everyone was here, some girls liked to hide themselves until the last moment, but judging from what she saw Aurora would win her pro card today.

Prejudging

Charles sat on his hands. He had to concentrate in order not to rock back and forth in his front-row seat. This was a disaster. The judges had finished with comparisons among the other contestants and were now focusing on the top three competitors. Aurora was one of them but she clearly was not the winner. Sheila Brooks stood two inches shorter than Aurora, had comparable size and symmetry, but was much leaner. She had the superior physique.

Charles leaned over, angry, and whispered in Hendrik's ear. "She might have had a chance if we'd lowered her carbs."

Hendrik pointed at Sheila Brooks. "I saw her two days ago. She was was ten pounds heavier. A waterlogged pig."

This information enraged Charles. "She probably soaked in Epsom salt baths." He watched the girls hit a side chest pose. "I wanted to do that." Charles rocked back and forth in his seat. "Why did I listen to you?"

Hendrik's answer was given in the most insulting of tones. "You think you can take ten pounds off in a bath?" He let out a harsh laugh, crossed his arms, and stared at the stage.

Charles was miserable. He wanted to take his Aurora and go

home. She'd win second place but second place meant nothing. There'd be no publicity. No pro card. Charles wanted to spit in Hendrik's face. When this was over it was back to Germany. Immediately. No question. Maybe Charles should arrange a drug possession charge. Send the idiot away for a few years. The thought made him smile. No, that could get messy. Best to get rid of him and start over. The U.S.A. was coming up next summer.

"It had to be Lasix." Hendrik spoke without turning to Charles. "They got really lucky."

Lasix was an injectable diuretic, very strong and hard to control. It was a dangerous drug and could turn a shredded muscular physique into a flat bag of bones in a matter of hours. Most bodybuilders used milder drugs like Aldactone or Diazide to rid themselves of excess water.

The judges called for a tricep shot and Charles' heart sank when he saw the deep separation in Sheila's arm. He wasn't sure that Aurora could have matched her even if she'd followed his plan. It was heartbreaking to see his girl up there smiling and proud. She had no idea that the girl standing next to her was superior. Sweet, dumb Aurora. He sank farther in his seat, defeated, and closed his eyes. He heard the head judge ask for a front double bicep but he didn't open his eyes. He couldn't bear the humiliation.

Charles had never failed with May. He'd chosen her contests carefully and, in her day, she was always triumphant. Perhaps he'd been too hasty in selecting Aurora. He could have done better if he'd waited. He should have traveled, seen what the country had to offer. There were a lot of good things coming out of Italy these days. And Germany, with all of those good Slavic genes.

"Look." Hendrik elbowed him, hard.

Charles opened his eyes and saw that Sheila was doubled

over with her hands on her knees. Aurora and the other girl, Mary Gail Bartz, stood firm in their front double bicep positions. Sheila straightened up, a pained grimace on her face, and resumed her pose but almost instantly dropped to her knees and curled in a ball.

Hendrik started to giggle. "There is a God in heaven."

"What's going on?" Charles could see that Sheila was having trouble breathing.

"She's cramping." Hendrik patted Charles' shoulder in excitement. "Too dehydrated. Muscles contract." He giggled again. "It could be fatal if the heart cramps."

Up on the stage, Aurora and Mary Gail looked confused but stayed in their double bicep poses while people rushed from the wings and knelt down by Sheila. Charles grabbed the seat back in front of him and leaned forward, his body tense. "Please don't let her get up," he prayed to himself.

The head judge yelled that someone should call an ambulance. People from the audience were rushing forward toward the stage. They bunched up in the aisles and shouted advice.

"Oxygen," a woman cried.

A group of people yelled in unison, "Get her some carbs."

Then a short, thick, muscular man with a shaved head and Fu Manchu beard, wearing a long black leather overcoat, stood on the seat behind Charles and screamed, "Sheila needs some some fucking water!"

A security guard ran out from backstage with a glass.

Hendrik put his hand on Charles' knee. "If she doesn't get up soon. That's it." He squeezed the knee hard. "Disqualified."

Sheila's body lay curled into a tight ball. She moaned with cries of deep agony. Three men lifted her body, rigid and fetuslike, and carried her off the stage. All the while Aurora and Mary Gail maintained their poses.

The head judge told Aurora and Mary Gail to relax while he

conferred with the other judges. The two girls hit the frontal relaxed position and waited, smiling brightly. The audience hurried back to their seats.

Hendrik leaned back, crossed his legs, and put his hands behind his head. He blew out a great lungfull of air and smiled. "That's it."

Charles leaned over, grabbed Hendrik's head, and kissed him on the mouth. "I told you we could do it."

Aurora the Pro

Aurora won her weight class and the overall title. She took home her pro card. She got a six-foot trophy made of etched wood and gold plastic and a certificate declaring her national champion. ESPN interviewed her. She had photo sessions scheduled for the next month. They promised her two magazine covers.

Those first few days after the show had been a hectic whirlwind with interviews and photographs. She hadn't had a chance to call home and give them the good news until Tuesday evening. Unfortunately, when she called, no one was there. Aurora left a message.

Charles said she should get off the drugs for twelve weeks. It was important that her body have a break from all the toxins. She would continue her training with Hendrik throughout the summer and then in September they'd start another cycle. Aurora didn't want to think about growing big again. She took one day at a time.

*   *   *

It was Thursday evening at nine o'clock when Aurora got home from the Muscle Mania photo shoot. Charles had been there all day, supervising her makeup and choice of posing suits. These were long days. The magazines wanted pictures of her doing lots of different exercises, in many different outfits and hairdos, so they'd have a large selection of photos. They got a year's worth of Aurora in one day.

The house was cold and dark when she came in. Aurora checked her answering machine and as usual there were no messages. She went upstairs, ran a bath, scrubbed the makeup off her face and soaked for twenty minutes.

All day, she'd had this feeling like she'd forgotten something. That feeling you get when you lock your keys in the car or leave your wallet on the counter at the supermarket. It was an irritating, almost panicky feeling, lurking there below the surface. She couldn't figure out what was missing. She knew exactly where her keys and wallet were.

Aurora got into bed and turned off the light. It was ridiculous to worry. She had everything she'd ever wanted. Aurora closed her eyes. There was an early photo shoot in the morning. She was going to get to ride a horse. Aurora went to sleep. She needed to look her best for tomorrow.

Charles' Next Step

One of the most fulfilling times of Charles' life was when May won her pro card. It felt like such an accomplishment. Such a thrill. Those frantic weeks following her success had been so exciting with all the interviews and pictures, the costumes and exotic locations. May had made quite a splash. Aurora was now getting comparable attention. She was scheduled for interviews and photo shoots with all the top magazines. She'd caught the attention of a talent agent who specialized in athletes. Soon she would be going out on commercial auditions. A chance to appear on TV was a bodybuilder's dream. Everything was going according to plan.

Charles accompanied Aurora on all her meetings and he longed for that same enthusiasm he'd felt with May. Every day he congratulated and encouraged Aurora, helped her with her hair and makeup, and played the roll of the proud sponsor. But it was all a fraud. Aurora would never have won if Sheila Brooks hadn't cramped onstage. Aurora was second best, a runner-up, and now Charles doubted her chances of success in the pro ranks.

The image of Sheila and Aurora onstage, just before Sheila doubled over, haunted Charles. Sheila Brooks. Charles rolled over and turned on the light. 11:45. He grabbed the phone and dialed Hendrik's private line.

"You have reached the answering machine taking messages for Mr. Hendrik von Got. Kindly leave a message at the tone."

"It's Charles."

Hendrik snapped up the phone. "Ja. What's happened?"

"Tell me about Sheila Brooks."

"What? They gave her some glucose, some water. She left hospital next afternoon."

"No. Who is she? Where does she live? How does she support herself?"

Hendrik paused. "Why, Charles?"

It infuriated Charles when Hendrik forgot his place, but tonight he kept his voice even and somewhat calm and said, "BECAUSE I WANT TO KNOW."

"She lives in Riverside. She's a personal trainer. Studying to become a nurse."

A nurse. Charles sat up in bed. A lovely muscular nurse. It was as if fate was delivering him his due. At last.

"Where does she train?"

"Not sure. Maybe the Powerhouse in Riverside."

"Find out. We're going to pay a visit."

Charles turned out the light, rolled over, and drifted off into a deep sleep.

Aurora Gives Her Liver a Break

The drugs, and Aurora's overwhelming ambition, had given her a set of binoculars in place of eyes. For almost a year, Aurora had looked through those binoculars at an image of herself on-stage, holding a first place trophy. There were few distractions; her focus had been absolute.

You had to slowly cycle off the steroids, and even when you stopped, it took a long time for the drugs to leave your system. It would be weeks before Aurora was "clean" but she could already feel the change. Her joints no longer ached and her muscles weren't as stiff. She was eating less food, losing a little weight, and her body felt light and healthy. She was more clear-headed. It wasn't good. Every morning when Aurora woke up, she had to face herself. As her body cleared, her mind flooded with the truth of what she'd done. Amy. She'd thrown away her daughter and pretended that it was for the best. A trophy, in trade, for her child.

And Skip was dead. He'd been an irritating, crazy man, but he'd never done anything to hurt Aurora and she now realized that he wouldn't have molested Amy. Not Skip. He was a troubled, confused person but he wasn't evil. He'd been a good friend to her at a time in her life when she had no direction. If it weren't for Skip, Aurora would never have become a bodybuilder. She owed him a lot when she walked out of his life, and she'd never had any intention of paying him back. Skip's death was an accident. Amy blamed Aurora for the death and some mornings Aurora thought that Amy was right.

The biggest challenge these days was getting out of bed. Aurora would wake in the morning and listen to the quiet emptiness of her house. The photo shoots and interviews, which at first had been so exciting, now felt like a tremendous burden. She didn't want to get up and shower. She didn't want to put on makeup. Fix her hair. Charles assured her that this was normal, a result of the chemical change combined with the letdown after a big contest. All bodybuilders went through this blue-transition.

Aurora's Big Break

Aurora put on the Fourth of July bikini Charles had delivered the night before. The bottoms were red and white striped, the top a dark blue with bursting white stars. Today was Aurora's first audition. She was up for a Ford commercial and they needed a girl in a bikini to pick up the back end of a truck. Charles said that the patriotic touch would give her an edge over the other girls.

All week, she'd practiced. Charles would hold the video camera and ask her to "slate" her name. Aurora would look right into the lens and say, with as much enthusiasm as she could, "I'm Aurora Johnson." She'd smile, tilt her chin, angle her shoulder, run her hands through her hair, flirt. Aurora Johnson, Aurora Johnson, Aurora Johnson. They'd do it twenty times, then plug into the TV and watch it back, until "Aurora Johnson" no longer sounded like her name but was just a sound she made to go with all her different faces.

The waiting room was filled with skinny beautiful fitness-girls. They were tall and shapely but had very little muscle. Some were in sweatpants, like Aurora, but most wore skimpy shorts with tight T-shirts that showed their sinewy little limbs. Aurora recognized a couple of bodybuilding girls from the gym and smiled, but none of them made eye contact.

All the seats were taken and Charles told Aurora to stand in the corner while he signed her in with the receptionist. She leaned against the wall and pretended to look for something in her purse in an attempt to hide her uneasiness.

Charles came back to join her and whispered, "Take off your sweats."

Aurora looked around again at all the bored and beautiful actresses. They'd obviously done this a million times. They were so cool and professional. Aurora took a deep breath and tried not to panic. The last thing she wanted to do was to draw attention to herself.

"Everyone else is dressed," she whispered to Charles in her softest voice. "I'll wait till I go in."

Charles raised his voice and hissed, "Do it."

Aurora felt herself blush through the thick layer of foundation makeup. Some of the other girls were watching her now. She buried her face deep in her purse as if there was some emergency in there.

"It'll give you an edge. There's no one here in your league." Charles took the purse gently out of her hands. "Trust me."

Aurora knew that Charles wouldn't change his mind. She had no choice but to obey him, otherwise he'd humiliate her by throwing one of his scenes. Charles always got his way. With hate burning through her body like acid, Aurora stripped down to her bikini and handed Charles her balled-up clothes. She folded her arms, leaned against the wall, and surveyed the room. Most of the girls had their heads down in a conspicuous effort to ignore her. Some of the more actressy girls had smirks on their faces. Aurora hated Hollywood.

The audition consisted of Aurora stating her name and pretending to lift an invisible pickup truck. They made her do it several times, facing the camera, in profile, a rear view. They encouraged her to make grunting sound effects and asked her how much she weighed. She heard someone whisper, "Steroids." The whole thing lasted less than five minutes.

Aurora dressed, then walked out into the waiting area. Charles was sitting next to a pretty Latin bodybuilder from the gym named Mimi Garcia. He was writing her number in his phone book and smiling his wormy little flirt-smile. Aurora walked past him and out to the parking lot as if she hadn't noticed. She felt more abandoned than jealous and tried hard not to cry as she waited for Charles to come out and take her home.

"How'd it go?" Charles unlocked her door.

Aurora got into the car and closed her door. She took a deep breath, trying desperately to be calm. Charles got in and she turned to him, opened her mouth to try to tell him that she never wanted to go on another audition again. That Hollywood was not for her. That she was an athlete and not an actress. But instead Aurora started to cry.

"Bad?" Charles started the engine. "The first ones often are. Don't worry, you'll get better at it."

Aurora shook her head and cried harder. She could feel that dangerous hysteria start to work itself free. Charles hated it when she cried but the more she tried to control herself the deeper she sank.

"Come on." Charles handed her a box of Kleenex. "It was just an audition."

Aurora blew her nose. "My mother won't answer the phone. I haven't talked to my daughter since she left. I've ruined everything." Part of Aurora separated and watched in amazement as the other part of her completely broke down. "I killed Skip."

Charles pulled his car off to the side of the road, turned off the engine, and faced Aurora. "What on earth are you talking about? You hate your mother. You paid absolutely no attention to that child. She was an unsupervised brat. And you were thrilled to get rid of her. She's exactly where she belongs."

Aurora didn't want him to be talking. She wanted him to take her home where it was quiet. She wanted silence. Home.

"As for that lunatic. It was an accident. You didn't kill him. And if you had, I would have applauded you. He was a nuisance and a child molester." Charles started the engine. "Now, snap out of it."

Aurora held her breath until the crying stopped. She'd have a nice bath and a nap when she got home. She'd call Hendrik and cancel her workout. She'd just go to sleep.

No Answer

On the bad days, no matter how many times Grandma said that it wasn't her fault, Amy couldn't get away from the guilt. She listened carefully to all of Grandma's words about accidents and fate and God's will, but none of those words could pull her out of the hopeless quicksand pit that she was stuck in. Little Amy was just a child, but little Amy had wanted something from Skip and Aurora knew it. If Aurora hadn't seen the need, the very adult love that Amy felt for Skip, he might still be alive. If Amy had just been more careful.

On the good days Amy pictured her mother in jail. Aurora's armorlike muscles would have melted away and she'd be stuck behind bars in the tiny cell, mourning the loss of her daughter and the death of a friend. Aurora would spend her life in that prison praying that Amy might visit from time to time. Praying for her daughter's forgiveness.

As the summer progressed, Amy was having more and more good days. She decorated her mother's prison cell with a sink and a filthy, diarrhea-stained toilet that was missing its seat. There were rats and cockroaches and the very bad smell of throw-up. The only foods available were potato chips and candy bars. Aurora's body grew fat and ugly. Amy would visit. They'd sit on opposite sides of the Plexiglas wall, talking on the phone. Aurora would press her hand to the glass and once again tell Amy how sorry she was.

Grandma and Amy never picked up the phone. Whenever it rang they'd rush to the den and stand by the answering machine, waiting to see who was calling. If Aurora was on the phone, lately she'd been calling more and more, they'd look at each other and pretend to consider picking up the receiver and then shake their heads and stand together listening to Aurora beg for news.

Today, Grandma was at the market when the phone rang. Amy stood by. She loved to hear her mother's increasing frustration at no one being home.

"Please pick up the phone." Aurora didn't sound angry today. She sounded sad. "Baby, I know you're angry with me. You've got every right to be."

Amy sat in the brown velour easy chair and watched the machine. She wished Grandma was home. Aurora was whining. Grandma would have loved it.

"I put you through hell these last few months." Aurora paused and blew her nose. "I wake up every morning regretting what I've done."

Bullshit. Amy wanted to knock the machine onto the floor. Just because her mother was having a tiny minute of regret, everything should be forgiven?

"I thought I was giving us a better life. California. All the money and the nice house. Things I thought you wanted. But I know now that all that was for me. You never cared about it. You're right. I am selfish. I was a monster."

Amy didn't like this. It was easy to hate her mother when she was a bitch but how was she supposed to feel now?

"And I'm sorry about Skip." Aurora started crying. "I think he was probably a good friend to you. Maybe the only one you had. I should never have accused him of those things. I'm so sorry that he's gone."

Amy started to cry too. The part of her that still wanted her mother, that still loved her, was breaking loose. She missed Skip. She missed her mama. Amy curled up in the chair and cried hard. It was so confusing. What was she supposed to do?

"Amy. I want you to know that I'll always love you. I made a mistake but I'm here for you now and I always will be."

Amy cried harder. She needed her mama there right now. She needed someone to hold her and tell her that everything would be all right. Someone to protect her.

"Baby, if you ever need me you just call."

Aurora hung up the phone and Amy stayed curled in a ball, crying in that easy chair until Grandma came back from the market.

A Letter from Grandma

Jeanine,

Do you think that your messages are helping? That Amy looks forward to hearing from you? Do you really think we care about your photo shoots and your interviews? That your career has any meaning to us? And do you believe, for one second, that that self-indulgent apology made your daughter feel BETTER?

You almost destroyed this beautiful child. When she came back with me she could barely function. She held on to my hand and wouldn't leave my side for weeks. She's better now. She's remembering the things in her life that bring pleasure. Amy's home. But your phone calls don't help. They remind her of what you've done. Of how little you cared. They hurt her.

If you have any love for this child, you'll leave her alone. Live your life in California and let us live ours. Please.

Your Mother

Climb Every Mountain

Charles sat in his living room, idly examining the antique globe. He would assemble a covey. A collection of women from around the world. Every ethnic group would be represented by the most superior bodybuilder from that country. He would have a stable of women. The Worthington girls. His champions. Slavic, Italian, rich dark African and icy Scandinavian. Charles could travel with them and conquer the globe.

It would take time. He would have to personally bring each girl along to a certain level of achievement, then turn her over to someone like Hendrik. It would be enormously time-consuming. The traveling and scouting. The intensive interviews. Charles took a deep breath. It excited him. He was made for this task.

Sheila Brooks was the first recruit and she had jumped at the chance to become one of his athletes. She knew of the arrangement with Aurora, apparently a lot of the girls did, and she found the terms quite favorable. Mimi, all fire and spice, was eager to join the group. His lovely brown Latina.

Sheila and Aurora were both Caucasian. Later, as the stable grew more crowded, he'd probably have to eliminate Aurora. Yes,

Aurora would have to go unless, of course, she surprised him and made tremendous gains throughout this year. For now, Charles thought the three girls could complement each other nicely. It tickled him to think of Sheila, Mimi and Aurora in nurses' uniforms tending to his needs. Sheila, Mimi and Aurora wrestling for his attention. Competing for his time. The possibilities were endless.

A True Friend

Aurora parked her car in the lot. She got out, grabbed her bag, hit the button on her car alarm and headed toward the gym. These functions were automatic, like blinking or breathing. Aurora didn't need to participate; her body took care of itself. And lately, she could go through an entire workout without thinking or focusing on what she was doing. Her mind wandered now, looking for something to latch on to. Training no longer brought her pleasure. Nothing did.

Hendrik was waiting for her today at the front desk. He smiled and waved as she walked through the door. It was unusual for him to be there but Aurora didn't care to wonder about it.

Hendrik put his arm around her shoulder and guided her into the gym. "You look good. Rested."

Aurora wished he'd take his arm off her shoulder. She didn't look good. She'd taken to wearing old sweatpants and T-shirts again. She hadn't washed her hair in days. Her body was tight and staying lean but no one would be able to tell that under all those clothes. What was Hendrik up to?

"I give you a little break today." He squeezed Aurora's shoulder and kissed her on the top of her head. "Nice, light workout."

Aurora pulled away from Hendrik. He never kissed her. In fact, they had very little physical contact. She didn't want his affection. "What's going on?"

"You're upset."

"No, I'm not." Aurora started walking toward the back of the gym. It was leg day.

"It doesn't bother you?" Hendrik had his hand on her shoulder again and stopped her from walking away.

Aurora was annoyed. She hated when Hendrik played his "surprise" games.

Hendrik shook his head. He looked very sad. "Charles didn't tell you." He grabbed her arm and guided her toward the exit. "Let's go outside."

Aurora yanked her arm away. She felt a jolt of fear. "What are you talking about?"

Hendrik took her hand and pulled her along. "Outside."

Hendrik led Aurora to his Cadillac. He unlocked the passenger door and held it open while she slid in. The car smelled strongly of the cardboard watermelon air freshener that hung from the rearview mirror. Aurora was heavy and tight with dread. Something bad was going to happen. How many more bad things could there be in a person's life? Amy was gone. She had no friends. She was a laboratory animal, a trained rat with nothing to look forward to. There wasn't much left to lose but still she felt scared. Aurora sat stiffly in the seat and braced herself. Hendrik hurried around the car and climbed in on the driver's side.

"I told him you'd be upset." Hendrik reached over and tried to take her hand but she pulled away.

Aurora felt very tired. She wanted this to be over. "Tell me."

"He was supposed to tell you." Hendrik shook his head. "This is not my job. I shouldn't have to."

The car was stuffy and the sickening-fruity smell made it hard for Aurora to breathe. "Please."

"He's taking on other girls." Hendrik gripped the steering wheel as he spoke. "There's two now but he's planning on more." He paused and looked out the windshield. "It won't affect us. I'll give you first priority." Hendrik looked Aurora in the eye. "You know that?"

Aurora nodded, not in agreement, but to keep him talking.

"He wants all the races. One of each." Hendrik shook his head and looked up at the moon roof. "He thinks he can control the world. Maybe someday start his own federation."

Aurora sat still and tried to understand. As much as she hated Charles she had thought their bond was solid. She thought of it as a complicated involvement where they needed and supported each other. She'd assumed that, sick as it was, theirs was a lasting relationship. They took care of each other. It was a sort of marriage. Aurora thought Charles loved her in his twisted way.

She took a deep breath. "Who does he have?"

"A girl from the gym. Mimi Garcia."

It hurt. Aurora could see Charles hunched over, writing her number in his black leather phone book. Right under her nose. She shouldn't have been surprised but she was.

"I start training her on Monday." Hendrik grabbed the steering wheel again and held on. "She'll be afternoons so you won't have to see her."

"Who else?" Aurora felt reckless. She could take it. Bring it on.

Hendrik sighed and didn't answer. People walked by the car and looked in. Joey, the gym manager, waved but Hendrik ignored him.

"It's okay," Aurora insisted. "I want to know."

Aurora looked at Hendrik. She thought she could see the beginning of tears in his eyes. He put his hand on her knee, squeezed gently, and said, "Sheila Brooks."

It was like jumping into ice water. You couldn't move, you

couldn't scream. Aurora thought she'd just sink to the bottom and drown. Sheila Brooks was the enemy. Their enemy. You never talk to the competition. Never associate with them. Sheila Brooks was the one they had to beat, the one Aurora did beat, and now Charles wanted her? How could he? Why? What did he need her for?

Aurora stared at the button on the glove compartment. This betrayal was so deep, it took her voice. She felt numb. They sat quietly and Aurora tried to think of options. Something she could do.

Hendrik leaned over the center console and pulled Aurora into a hug. She leaned into him and started to cry on his shoulder. The smell of his Old Spice was comforting. It was familiar and safe. Hendrik was loyal. He was her friend.

Through her tears she said, "I thought he loved me."

Hendrik let go of her and reached behind him to the backseat for a box of Kleenex.

Aurora blew her nose, then cried even harder. "All those things I've done for him. Sick stuff. It isn't fair." She was dizzy with her pain.

"Ja. He has not treated you well." Hendrik took a roll of Wintergreen Life Savers from the center console and offered one to Aurora. She took it and chewed it up like a potato chip. The crunching noise inside her head was comforting. She took another.

"You don't have to put up with this," Hendrik said.

"What can I do? He owns me. Everything." It was hopeless.

"You could walk away." Hendrik looked her in the eye.

Aurora shook her head. That wasn't an option. How would she support herself?

"I have a little business," Hendrik said. "A side venture. You could work for me."

"What are you talking about, Hendrik?" Aurora looked at

her sweet, loyal friend. "Your jewelry?" There was no way he could generate enough income on that horrible stuff he made to support them both. And Aurora definitely did not want to get involved with dealing drugs.

Hendrik reached under his seat, pulled out a magazine, and handed it to Aurora. It was thick, like a fashion magazine, and there was a bodybuilder on the cover in a leather teddy. The magazine was called *Delux*. Aurora opened to the first page and saw a picture of Angel Ray, former Ms. Olympia, on a stairway, straddling a carved mahogany banister. There was a big stained-glass window in the background that gave the place a sacred feeling, but the look on Angel's face said *dirty sex*. Aurora flipped to the next page. Julie Holmes in a black leather thong and a chain bra that showed her nipples.

Aurora dropped the magazine in Hendrik's lap, disgusted and a little bit scared. "What is this?"

"It's my company. The girls hire out for wrestling and what-not. They make very good money. You would be very popular."

Aurora felt sick. Nothing was what it seemed. She grabbed her gym bag and got out of Hendrik's car. Hendrik was a pimp? He wanted her to become one of his whores? She walked over to her car and got in. Hendrik followed but she ignored him. She didn't want to listen to the explanation. She knew everything she needed to know. Aurora started her car and drove home.

Everything That She Needs

Aurora walked in the front door of her house and saw that there was a message on the answering machine.

"We're having a little party." Charles chuckled. "A chance for us all to get acquainted. Tomorrow night at seven o'clock. Wear the cheerleader outfit. Make those nice big freckles and of course no panties." He giggled. "Don't be late."

Aurora felt very calm as she listened to Charles' voice. Clear-headed. Happy even. She had realized, when she drove away from Hendrik, that she could drive away from anything. No one could make her live this life. She had a choice.

Aurora walked upstairs and into her bedroom. She didn't need much. Didn't really want much of what she had here anyway. She took out a suitcase and packed some clothes. Jeans, T-shirts. Basic clothes. There was ten thousand dollars in her personal checking account. She had a credit card that she planned to use until Charles canceled it.

Aurora carried the suitcase out to her car. She wasn't sure which direction she'd drive but all roads led to somewhere else. Aurora couldn't lose.

She went back into the house. There was one last thing she had to take care of.

Aurora Finally Comes Through

Charles was having a delightful afternoon. The handyman had done a beautiful job with the world map. It fit perfectly on the wall behind the posing platform. Eight feet high and ten feet long, it was mounted like wallpaper. Charles was pleased that he hadn't had to sacrifice Greenland. There was plenty of room. The nice blues of the oceans, the greens and browns of the continents, lent a cheery air to the room. His world headquarters.

Charles stuck a pin with a tiny blue flag in Southern California to represent Sheila. He put a red flag in the center of Mexico, near the capital, for Mimi. Aurora had a yellow flag in Georgia. He looked forward to the day when this map was dense with colorful markers.

Aurora's phone call had come as a complete shock. Charles had expected some resistance to his idea. Jealousy. He'd been ready to cut her loose. Send her back to Georgia. But she called to accept his plan and said that she'd be a team player. Then, in a move that took Charles' breath away, she asked to come over. She wanted to be alone with him one more time before she became part of a group. Said she had a surprise. Charles couldn't believe this happy change. It thrilled him that she was finally taking the initiative

The doorbell rang and Charles rushed downstairs to answer. Aurora stood with her legs shoulder width apart, arms down at her sides, muscular and hard. She was dressed in tight black vinyl pants and matching halter. Her five-inch black leather pumps were cruelly pointed. There was a hunting knife in a black leather holster strapped to her left calf. She held a bullwhip in her left hand and a black leather suitcase in her right. Charles swooned. He himself couldn't have come up with a more electrifying vision.

"Aurora, I'm so proud of you." He moved back into the house and awaited her instructions. She was finally going to dominate him. He'd been wanting this for so long. Begging for it in his way. Sweet Aurora.

Aurora walked into the house. "Upstairs."

Charles paused. He wanted to break out of character, just for a moment before they began, and thank her. He wanted to tell her that this was his dream come true. That he'd always known she had it in her. He'd recognized her hidden strength. He'd always believed in her. He wanted to tell her that she'd always be his number one girl. All she'd needed was a little competition.

Aurora cracked her whip and knocked the antique Chinese vase off the table in the entry hall. It fell to the floor and shattered. "Move." Her voice was deep and menacing.

Charles felt a glimmer of fear travel up his spine. He ran toward the stairs, thrilled by the danger. The vase was five hundred years old. Priceless.

She followed him up the stairs. "Get the cane chair."

He ran down the hall to his room and got the chair. What

was she up to? Charles had to be careful not to smile. Mustn't displease the mistress.

When he came into the posing room, Aurora told him to put the chair in the middle of the platform and to take off all of his clothes. She stood watching him as he disrobed. She looked angry, mean. Charles loved it. He wondered what she thought of the new map. Had she noticed her little flag? Charles started to fold his clothes.

"Sit in the chair!"

Charles dropped his clothes in a heap and hurried up onto the platform. Aurora took from her bag a roll of hairy brown twine. She forced Charles down into the chair, then started to tie his hands behind his back.

"Aurora, hon. I've got some nice velvet rope in the top drawer by the sink."

"Shut up."

Charles could tell right away that she was tying his wrists too tightly. She impaired his circulation and that could get very uncomfortable. Well, it was her first time. He decided not to say anything. Charles wanted to be supportive. It was important that this go well and she feel proud. Later he could gently point out the mistakes.

Aurora came around in front and tied his ankles to the legs of the chair. She used her sharp knife to cut the twine. Aurora's strong hand, gripping that knife, was stunning. Charles' penis stood tall in a full salute to her beauty.

"How do you like the chair, Charles?" Aurora stood in front of him, looking down. "Notice how the edges poke when your butt hangs through? You were going to fix that for me, remember? You never did."

Aurora pulled her weight belt out of her bag. "Gotta make sure you don't cheat. No lifting your hips." She looped the belt under the chair and cinched it down hard on Charles' lap, catching a bit of his scrotum in the buckle.

Charles cried out in pain.

"Pinches?" Aurora laughed and walked out of the room.

Actually, Charles felt quite uncomfortable. His sac was twisted by the buckle and his buttocks were falling through the hole in the chair, the cane bitting at his thighs and hips. He knew that Aurora meant this to be exciting but the discomfort diminished the erotic effect. He might have to intercede or this could turn into a disaster. His hands felt cold and numb. Charles was losing his erection. Poor, clumsy Aurora.

Aurora came back into the room carrying his vegetable dolls. "I brought your little friends." She dropped them in a pile near Charles' feet, then took from her bag a can of lighter fluid and a book of matches. She squirted the lighter fluid on the heap of dolls.

"STOP!" Charles couldn't believe his eyes. Those were his mother's dolls. She'd bought them in Spain sixty years ago. They were one of a kind. "What are you doing?"

Aurora stopped squirting the dolls and got a roll of duct tape out of her bag. "You talk way too much." She ran a long piece of tape over Charles' mouth, then went back to squirting the dolls.

"We're going to have a little barbecue." She stood back, lit a match, and threw it at the dolls.

There was an explosion of blue flame. Charles could feel the heat burn at his toes and curl the hairs on his shins. He was suddenly worried. This was obviously not sex play. He sat there helpless and watched while the flames died down and his precious treasures smoldered and burned.

Aurora watched the fire too. When it was no more than a smoking heap of fabric and melted plastic, Aurora said, "Time for your shots, Charles."

This woman was crazy. As soon as Charles was freed he'd have to make arrangements. Psychiatric ward for the criminally insane.

Aurora walked over to the cabinet and took out an armful of drugs. She carried them over and arranged them in front of his chair in a semicircle. She went back for two more trips until the cabinet was empty and the drugs were set up around him in neat rows. She opened a needle and scraped the tip across the floor, inserted it into one of the steroid bottles, and filled the syringe. "Gee, Charles. This might hurt a little bit. The needle's awful dull." Aurora walked behind Charles, lay down on the floor, and scooted under the chair.

Charles felt like he was being branded. Aurora stuck his exposed ass, from underneath the chair, with the dull needle and flooded him with a burning dose of steroids. Normally the drug would be administered slowly but she forced it in so fast he thought his skin would explode. He could feel that she'd left the needle hanging there when she got to her feet.

"Oh, Charles. You've lost your erection. Shriveled up little dick." Aurora frowned and looked at Charles' crotch. Then she smiled and said, "I can take care of that." Aurora walked over and picked up her knife, which was lying next to the smoking dolls.

Charles stared at her in horror.

Aurora walked over and ran the knife lightly across his neck.

Charles felt the wetness of his urine run down between his thighs. He'd never known such terror.

"Oh, you've wet yourself." Aurora grinned at him with a demonic smile. "I didn't mean to scare you. I'm not going to cut it off, I'm going to fix it."

Aurora went to the cabinet and took out another needle. She came back to the platform, got down on her knees, and started reading the labels of the drugs. "Pump n Pose. Remember how you shot this into my biceps? And how they stayed pumped and sore for two weeks? I didn't like that but you said it made me look so much better. Let's see what happens when I shoot this in your penis."

Charles heard himself whimper. It was a sound over which he had no control.

Aurora loaded the syringe, grabbed him, and stuck the needle right into the head of his penis. The searing pain was so bad that Charles wished he would faint. He couldn't breathe. Then his penis inflated like one of those long curly balloons they sold at the circus, blown up too fast by an overly powerful air compressor. It was twice its normal erect size and bursting with blood. He was sure that at any minute it would split open, like the blistered skin of a hot dog on a grill, and he would bleed to death.

"Charles, look what happened." Aurora stood over him. "I bet that hurts, huh?"

Charles nodded vigorously. There were tears running down his cheeks and he was moaning. He'd never known such pain.

"I better get some help." Aurora rushed over to the phone by the sink. "Did you know 911 gets you an ambulance, the fire department, and the police?"

Charles shook his head violently. "No, no, no, no," he yelled through the duct tape.

Aurora picked up the phone and dialed. Charles was horrified when he heard her scream, "Help! Help! There's an intruder in the house. Help!"

Aurora dropped the receiver and left it dangling. She picked up her bag and her whip, stepped off the platform, smiled at Charles and walked out the door.

AUTHOR'S NOTE

This novel started out as a short story about Aurora, Charles and Amy. I was interested in the dynamic between the three characters and kept writing about them until a novel started to materialize. That the book takes place in the world of woman's bodybuilding was initially of secondary importance, but as the novel progressed so, too, did my interest in writing about the sport. It is a subject I've been thinking about for many years.

I was a competitive bodybuilder—a little one with really small muscles. I won the 1992 Southern California Bodybuilding Championship but was never even near the level of the girls I write about in *Chemical Pink*. I have, however, been training at Gold's Gym Venice since the early eighties, know the bodybuilding world well, and have always been fascinated by the people who devote their lives to this sport.

Everybody knows that bodybuilders use steroids. Take a walk through Gold's and you will see a lot of women with pronounced secondary male characteristics. Though my account is fictionalized, everything I have written in this book can—and has—happened. I never took drugs and as a result competed on a much lower level than Aurora. But women do take these drugs and suffer from these side effects. Once you grow facial hair or a penis-like clitoris you are stuck with it for the rest of your life, even if you stop taking the drugs. You're always going to have that deep voice. Most troubling is the fact that because steroids are a controlled substance, and no one admits that they're using, very little research has been done about the long-term effects on women. We can see what's happening externally, but it's hard to know what's going on internally and how it may affect long term health.

When I started to write about this rarefied world, it was important to me that the drug-related details be absolutely accurate and so I consulted two of the best-known experts in this field. Both men have had a lot of experience training women and writing "supplement" programs for them. With their help, I came up with a training and drug schedule that someone like Charles might use with Aurora. Then I met with each man separately, on a weekly basis, and we took Aurora through this program, imagining what would be happening to her day by day.

People ask me why a woman would want to do these things to her body. Before I answer that I want to make it very clear that I think weight training and natural bodybuilding is one of the healthiest things a person can do. It's good for you to build muscle and it is psychologically very empowering to have a strong body. I train almost every day and probably will for the rest of my life. I think everyone can benefit from time in the gym.

However, competitive bodybuilders—on the level described in the book—are obviously extremists. Sometimes, some of them lose sight of what's really happening in their bodies and in their lives. The only thing that matters at that point is getting bigger, harder, and leaner regardless of the consequences. There is always someone in the gym encouraging the bodybuilder to take it to the next level; "Try this new drug, don't worry about tomorrow." You see this same self-destructive behavior in other sports: the ballet dancer who starves herself and ruins her body for a career that will certainly be over before she hits thirty; the football player who continues to play with a serious injury even though he knows he may be crippled for life. Athletes in many

different sports use steroids now. Consequences aren't important—all that matters is winning.

Chemical Pink is a story about obsession and drive within a
small subculture but, if you take a step back, the book reflects
the narcissistic priorities of today's culture.